A LOVE SONG FOR ALWAYS

RIVALS #4

PIPER LAWSON

1

Annie

"Can't we move any faster?" I lean toward the partition between the front and back seats of the limo. "There must be another road. Let me check."

The driver shoots me a patient look. "Miss Jamieson, it's the 405."

From the seat next to me, Rae laughs silently. "Forgive her. She has a serious case of Tyler Adams withdrawal caused by spending too much time apart from her hot fiancé."

Since I jumped out of bed in New York this

morning ahead of the five-thirty alarm to shower and dress, every part of me has been buzzing with anticipation.

Most of my day was spent on the flight to LA with Rae, but I was too distracted to work or read.

Now, the stop-and-go traffic makes me want to roll down my window and shout at the world. Instead, I drum my fingers on the bare knee I nicked my second time over it with a razor.

"Seriously. I don't need to crash with you and Tyler while I play my gigs this week," Rae goes on.

"Yes, you do. There are five bedrooms." Tyler took me on a virtual tour before he rented the house before our wedding. It gave him a home base to work on album release promotions with the studio until I could hand my Broadway role to another actress so Tyler and I could have the next month together before his tour. "Even when Dad and Haley show up with the kids tomorrow, that leaves plenty of space."

Traffic breaks, and the car surges toward the exit.

Yes.

"Did you see the news about Wicked Records?" Rae holds up an article on her phone about my Dad's former label.

I resolve to focus and not degenerate into a throbbing ball of need now that my fiancé is only minutes away.

"Sounds like after years of mismanagement, they're going down fast. Dad hasn't been involved with them for a long time. Not since he was fighting over his songs."

"Have he or your stepmom said anything?"

"Not to me." But we haven't exchanged more than a rushed voicemail or emails with wedding logistics in the better part of a month given how busy things have been preparing for this time off.

My finger drumming on my knee starts again.

"Just as well you're dropping me at the club so I won't be there when you see Tyler," Rae offers. "I don't want to be within earshot when you guys... *reunite*." She enunciates each syllable.

There's no point trying to hide the flush that crawls up my face.

I have been anticipating all the parts of seeing my fiancé. Not only because we're getting married in a week, but because I haven't kissed him, touched him, or shared more than a sexy FaceTime call with him in a month.

I've been in love with Tyler Adams for a decade, long before he became a rock star and I wrote a Broadway show.

Now we're about to tie the knot.

The obstacles that kept us apart felt insurmountable at the time. But our love, our tenacity, and maybe a little destiny kept bringing us back to one another. Next weekend is validation of all we've been through.

"I grew up wanting to be on stage, but the whole bride fantasy skipped me," I admit.

"No parade with stuffed animals down a made-up aisle?"

I shake my head. "But the moment Tyler and I decided on a date, it was like something took me over. I wanted all of it. The guests. The dress. The cake. The music."

"The man," she finishes.

And what a man.

I swore I'd never fall for a rock star. Growing up with my dad's fame rubbed me the wrong way. I felt I had to prove myself—to him and to everyone. It took years for me to realize I belonged, that I could carve my own path without being lessened by his or jealous of Tyler's relationship with my dad.

"Our lives have been anything but perfect. This week will be the exception," I confide.

Our destination wedding will take place on a stunning island with private beaches and exquisite accommodations. After, Tyler and I have cleared our schedules for nearly a month. There'll be nothing but relaxation and enjoy newly wedded bliss with my best friend, who also happens to be my fiancé and the hottest guy on the planet.

I've been planning it with crazed fervor.

To be clear, perfect doesn't mean glossy-magazine-worthy. It's about having time with each other and the people we love in a beautiful, private place that feels like heaven.

The car pulls up at the club, and Rae gets out before leaning in the open window. "Do me a favor and put a sock on the door if you're not done when I get back."

"Does anyone even own socks in LA?" But I wave, and the car pulls off again.

As we take the streets up into the Hills, excitement thrums low in my stomach. Tyler's been finishing his album to earn the month off for our wedding before he goes on tour. Even while living together in New York for most of a year, I didn't feel as though we had time together because we were doing eight shows a week. It was a thrilling and exhausting grind, but we decided to move him out of the lead role a few months after it started on Broadway so he could finish his album.

Now I want him to myself.

I check my phone for Tyler's texts from when I left this morning.

Annie: Can't wait to see you.

Tyler: Can't wait to taste you.

My thighs press together under my short, black dress. I could text Tyler to say we're a few minutes away.

But that would ruin the surprise.

Instead, I put on a song from his new album. His voice wraps around me, raw and sexy and the kind of earnest that makes fans go crazy.

By the time the driver pulls up, passing two parked Rolls and a Maserati on the road before turning into the gates and entering the passcode I gave him, I'm so turned on it's dangerous. The gates swing wide, and I get a clear look at the house. It's stunning, white and modern with high trees surrounding it for privacy.

The driver leaves my bags at the door at my request. The garage is open, revealing a black Lambo the owners left and a motorcycle. I bought the bike for Tyler as a gift. I hunted for ages for the vintage Triumph Bonneville. I'd considered having it fixed up before I gave it to him, but I knew he'd want to fix it himself. A way to blow off some steam.

Now it's pristine.

I trail a hand along the chrome and the leather

seat in appreciation. The things my guy can do with his hands...

I open the door and step inside. My wedge sandals click on the marble as I steady my racing heart.

"That bike is hot," I call, pushing my sunglasses onto my head and scrunching a hand through the long, red hair I hope is still wavy after a day on the plane.

"If only I could find someone to take me on it."

The evidence of my arousal fills every syllable as I step out into the living room.

"And when I say, 'Take me'? I mean..."

I trail off, my throat tightening.

The man I love stands in the center of the vast room, seeming to fill the entire space with his presence.

Tyler Adams is breathtaking in profile. As gorgeous as ever in dark jeans that cling to his lean hips and strong legs, a white T-shirt that pulls across his chest and shoulders, revealing black ink that curls down his arm all the way to his fingers. His dark hair falls over his face, and when he turns to face me fully, he shoves it back.

The light from the floor-to-ceiling windows streams across his tan face, his cut jaw, and the firm mouth that tastes better than anything on this planet.

Tyler's heavy chocolate gaze locks on mine, holding me prisoner.

But it's his guilty expression that has me stunned.

And the fact that he's not alone.

2

Tyler

When a man asks a woman to be his wife, he shouldn't have to be without her again. But life doesn't obey "shoulds," and for the past month, I've been working on promotions for my new album in LA while she wrapped up handing off her show in New York.

Being forced to live apart from the person you love means you devote a lot of energy to reunion fantasies.

In the hours between finishing my album, Annie and I have reunited on the marble kitchen counter. The walk-in-closet-sized shower. The hot tub. The pool.

Fuck, have we reunited in the pool...

None of my fantasies had her staring at me like this.

"What's going on?" She's frozen in the doorway like some beautiful woodland creature realizing it wandered to the wrong stream to drink. Color has her cheeks pink under the trace of freckles. Her black dress skims curves I know in exquisite detail, leaving her shoulders bare and ending midway down the toned thighs I could spin endless fantasies out of, especially when they're wrapped around me.

"You're early," I say.

Looking past me, she surveys the suits who're covering their notepads and computers.

"It's okay," I tell them.

Only then do they relax an inch. I turn back to my fiancée and close the distance between us in a few easy strides. She smells as good as she looks, and I want to bury my face in her neck.

And then other places.

I've seen every expression Annie Jamieson owns, and with a few exceptions—like the way she looks when I've ripped her heart in two, which I swear I'll never witness again—I love them all. But in this moment, there are few things I wouldn't give to replace her look of stunned suspicion with one of wanton pleasure.

"These are my attorneys," I say, covering up my desires. "We're working up an agreement."

She cocks her head, amber eyes flashing. "It's a little late to talk about a prenup."

I'd laugh if she didn't look so alarmed.

My gaze strokes over the curve of her full lower lip, wishing I could feel it rather than stare at it. "It's not a prenup. I'm buying Wicked."

She stiffens, turning before I kiss her so my mouth grazes her cheek instead.

Annie heads to the kitchen.

I hold up a finger to let the lawyers know I'll be a second before following her. She sidesteps around boxes of merchandise I'm supposed to sign for my upcoming tour, and I avoid them too.

Near the giant stainless smart fridge, she turns. "You're *what*?"

This is not how I wanted this to happen.

"Your dad's been working on a deal since he heard they were at risk of going under. Quietly."

Something clicks behind her eyes. "He's been trying to get hold of me, but we've been playing phone tag. Since when are you involved?"

"He needed additional partners."

"You mean your money."

"Yes. We've been discussing it for a few weeks—"

"Not with me." Her voice is sharp, but there's an edge of hurt underneath. I hate that I put it there.

Annie Jamieson experiences the world full throttle. It's one of the things I love about her. It fucking ruins me how raw she is, and it makes me want to protect her—from the world and from herself when she feels *everything*.

"I wanted to tell you in person."

Annie and I have talked about the need to make investments, even though we've discussed our finances before and agreed—technically, she insisted—most of our money would be kept separate. She's so damn independent and doesn't want to owe anyone, including me, anything.

(Of course, the day we're married, her name goes on everything whether she wants it or not. There's no way I'm not taking care of her if and when she needs it.)

"So, you're going to run a label?" Her voice rises.

"Fuck no," I say firmly, reaching for her arms.

This reunion is going nothing like it was supposed to. Her body should've been under mine by now. Judging by the words she uttered before she walked in, she wanted that too.

Now she's pissed, and I'm horny, and we're fighting in the kitchen with half a dozen lawyers who charge for an hour what I used to make in a month listening from the other room.

I wanted to keep her out of this deal because I didn't want her worrying about it, or me, or the fact that Jax and I are doing it together. Annie and her dad have had enough issues in the past, and some of them have been my fault. He's not only my future father-in-law, but my mentor. The man who helped put me on the map.

But I swore I wouldn't come between them again, which is why I insisted to Jax I wanted a transactional deal: my money and reputation as someone without any grudges in the industry in exchange for a share of one of the biggest record companies of all time.

And it was supposed to be finished by now.

Frustration has me biting back a groan.

"It's an investment," I say evenly. "That's all."

Still, Annie looks unconvinced. "I know the new album is doing well, but that's why you have an investment manager. Buy a horse ranch or a vineyard or something."

I take her hand, threading my fingers through hers. "Six... I'd have to buy more than one."

"Oh."

God, I love this woman. She grew up with nothing. Then she learned her father was Jax Jamieson, and she was transplanted into a world with *everything*. She never takes a piece of it for granted.

I swear I never will either.

"Wicked has a lot of up-and-coming talent," I say.

"Talent that will suffer if the company goes under, and they don't deserve that."

There's another reason I want a piece of this deal, one that matters even more for our future. It's been emerging for months, brewing in the back of my mind as she slept beside me, finally maturing in the weeks I've been without her.

But I'm not ready to cop to it yet.

Annie sighs, her head falling back to stare at the ceiling. "We're getting married in seven days," she starts, and I sense she's thawing.

"Believe me, I remember." I inch closer, and her back bumps the fridge. "On an island. All our friends and family flying to—"

"Don't say it! You'll jinx it!" She presses a finger to my lips.

My mouth twitches beneath her touch. No money or shit in the world can hold a candle to Annie Jamieson. She's my friend, my rival, my heart. The only woman I've ever loved, the only person I've wanted to own or be owned by.

"I promise I won't risk our time together for this deal," I vow, tracing my thumb along her palm until she shivers.

I nip her finger, and her lips part. My hand releases hers to skim up her side under the edge of her dress, and she shifts against the fridge, which beeps.

She jumps, but I don't let her shift away. My mouth brushes her ear, and I inhale her scent like an addict. "Give me twenty minutes to get rid of the lawyers."

Annie ducks out of my arms, smoothing down her dress and leveling me with a stare. "Take your time. I'm going swimming."

The cool challenge in her eyes only adds to my lust. I want to drag up her skirt and claim her right here.

"Twenty minutes," I promise, but she's already brushing past me and heading for the bedrooms.

I adjust myself in my jeans before returning to the conversation in the living room.

"Let's wrap this up," I tell the lawyers when I return and sit on the edge of the sofa. No point getting comfortable.

"We have one week before the exclusivity clause lapses, which means the company goes back on the market," the lead attorney says. "Problem is the exec-utive team is carrying more debt than they disclosed."

"So get us an accurate version," I say, irritated. When I signed on, I figured the dozens of attorneys and advisors would handle the details, but things are turning out to be anything but easy.

"We're working on it. But even if we get a complete accounting…" One of the lawyers looks up and trails off.

I turn in my seat to follow his gaze out the doors to the patio.

Marrying your best friend is a blessing and a curse. She knows your dreams, your ambitions, your secrets.

She also knows your weaknesses.

My fiancée, still in her high-heeled sandals, appears from the direction of the master bedroom.

In a purple bathing suit and a wispy cover-up that covers zero fucking things up, she's a witch. A siren. A magnetic north pole.

She tugs off the cover-up and tosses it on a chair. Then she bends over, unfastens her shoes, and steps out of them.

Ignoring every male gaze on her, she takes one step at a time down into the pool, then dives, reappearing a moment later. Her copper hair is darkened and hanging in a wet curtain down her back.

A vein pounds in my forehead as I rise, dragging my gaze back to the lawyers. "We'll pick this up tomorrow."

The lead attorney shifts forward. "But, Tyler, we need to finish reviewing the—"

"Later. You can see yourselves out." My tone is final as I reach for my belt with one hand and turn my back on them. "I have a prior engagement."

3

Annie

I'm lying on my back, the water lapping around my ears and the sun warming my body, when a shadow falls over me. I blink my eyes open and right myself, frowning as I look back over one shoulder toward the living room.

No more heads of the lawyers poking above the sleek minimalist furniture.

I turn back to the view, the carefully designed illusion that the pool edge hangs off the Hollywood Hills and looks down on the valley of West Hollywood. But it's not the view that has me hypnotized. It's the man standing at the top of the carved steps at one end of the pool.

He's tall and strong, every part of him built with intention, from his carved torso and arms to his lean hips and the perfect ass I can't see from here but could draw from memory.

From fifteen feet away, he feels my blatant perusal.

He expects it.

"Lawyers left for nap time?" I call.

Tyler strips off his shirt in a single movement.

His body is art. A canvas of lean muscle and tattoos I know as well as I know any part of my own body.

His attention is on me, as if the view, the house, the pool, all mean nothing. He walks down the steps into the pool, the water soaking his jeans. He doesn't look down once, not when it claims his waistband, licks at his abs.

My thighs clench under the water.

I should tell him he's getting wet, that we're not cool after what went down inside, but I'm riveted by the look in his eyes.

I can't do anything but let the water ripple around me, the hairs lifting on my arms and neck as he approaches, my nipples pebbling just above the water level. My heart hammers at his closeness, my palm flattening against the heated skin of his chest.

He frowns. "Where's your ring?"

I nod toward the side of the pool. I didn't want to lose it, to have the pool chemicals affect it. It's there along with my necklace and the promise ring he got me before we split up for his tour.

Tyler wades across the pool to retrieve both.

My breath catches as he reaches for my hand beneath the water. He doesn't lift it out, just slips the diamond ring over my fingertip. The metal and his touch are whisper-light along my skin, a sexy, possessive slide that ends in firm pressure as the band slides home.

He murmurs in my ear, "You're mine."

"You think I need a ring to remember that?" I tease.

"No. You remembered it every time we hung up on a video call this past month. Every time I told you what I'd do to you if we were together. But it's not the same." He wraps the necklace around my neck and uses it to tug me forward until our lips are almost touching.

A thrill works through me.

I'm mad at him. He knows it, but it's harder when he's this close.

I force a shrug. "Your billboard in Times Square kept me company."

The crinkling at the corners of his eyes cracks my resolve. His thumb brushing my lips doesn't help either.

"Too bad." His beautiful voice breaks. "Because I

fucking missed you, Annie Jamieson."

His arms band around me as he crushes my body to his.

Yes.

Tyler's mouth is hard and demanding, as if everything he's owed is on the other side of my lips and he won't stop until he's claimed it all.

The broken prince I fell for, the relentless man he became, they twine together. I belong to both of them, both of him.

The dirty thoughts that've been taking me over since I woke up this morning. Every part of me cries out for this, for him.

My back hits the side of the pool, and I suck in a surprised breath. I didn't know we were moving. I was focused on his cedar scent sending me reeling, the possessiveness of his mouth slanting over mine, the hard denim of his jeans abrading my stomach and thighs.

Tyler lifts me up on the edge of the pool, breaking our kiss to stare at me with wide pupils under a thick fringe of lashes.

He drags my hips to the edge, and I fall back on my hands. My core—wet from his touch, not the water—presses against his abs, separated from him only by the thin fabric of my bikini bottoms.

"I know what you're trying to do," I manage.

"Make me forgive you with sex."

His slow grin could steal hearts and panties at once. "Is it working?"

I loop my arms around his neck, feathering his hair as I look down. "Tyler, I'm serious. I don't even know where to start."

"My jeans are wet. You could start with those."

I slap a hand against his shoulder. "Dammit. I wanted you. I thought I'd walk in and everything would be good and..."

His jaw works, guilt flaring behind his dark eyes. "I'm sorry, Six. I hoped it would be done by the time you got here. Now, I could spend the next hour *telling* my future wife I fucked up, or I could show her how much I missed her in the little time we have before your dad and Haley and the kids arrive tomorrow."

His hot, purposeful mouth travels down my neck, lingering along my collarbone, where he knows it makes me shiver, and sends a tendril of heat straight to my core.

I'm so entranced by his words I almost forget. "Half an hour."

"Hmm?"

"I promised I'd meet Beck this afternoon. He said he had a surprise."

"Fuck Beck."

"He's your best friend," I remind him.

Tyler eliminates every millimeter of space between us, pressing his tight abs against my heat and inviting me to rub on him as his mouth moves lower. "If he keeps you away, the man is dead to me."

He massages my breast with his hand, lifting it so his tongue skims along the edge of one cup.

He's not holding me against him anymore, but I couldn't move away if I tried. I'm already on fire when he lifts my breast out of the top and sucks on an already-peaked nipple, sending a bolt of need through me.

I yank on his hair hard enough it should hurt. He doesn't make a sound, just touches me, licks me, grazes his teeth over my sensitive skin until I'm reduced to a pile of wanting.

Out of nowhere, I remember New Year's Eve. We spent it apart but on a video call, each of us retreating to the roof so we could stare at the same sky.

"Your memory will keep me warm until you're back," I told him.

"I've never left. My heart is with you."

We talked for hours, wishing for time, for space. For this moment.

I swallow, fighting the wave of emotion in my chest. I don't want some quickie in the few minutes we have. But it's all I'm going to get.

He yanks on the string at the side of my bikini, and the fabric gives way, baring me to his view.

With a knowing look, he moves down my body. "What's that smile?" His mouth vibrates against my skin in a way that makes me tremble.

"Rae said to leave a sock on the front door."

"We're not in college anymore," he reminds me. As if I need a reminder he's not the boy I grew up with, but a man. "This is my house, and I will fuck my fiancée until she screams. I don't care who hears."

I'm breathless even before his tongue paints a line down my wet slit.

My fingers dig into his hair and the sight before me steals not only my oxygen, but my need for it.

The skyline of Hollywood, Sunset, and the surrounding streets, stretching to the ocean.

My rebel prince. His hand—the one dark with ink, with roses and swirls—traces up the inside of my thigh, higher and higher, as he devours me.

Heat rolls over me in a consuming wave. It's not the sun or the balmy air, but Tyler's relentless mouth lighting fires in every nerve.

I want to take this slowly, but I'm too over-whelmed. My heart and my body feed off each other, off him, and when he sucks right above where his fingers are playing, I break apart like a wave on the shore.

It's not enough. Nowhere near.

When I come down from the climax, I shift forward, reaching for the button on his jeans.

But Tyler bats my hand away.

"Later." His raspy voice is a promise. "We have plans after you're done with my ex-best friend."

"You want me to wait," I echo, already aware of the emptiness between my thighs now that his fingers have gone.

A smile ghosts across his face as he reaches for the strings on my bikini bottoms, fastening one side, then the other.

"This pout." His lips brush over mine, and I can taste myself on his tongue. "I forgot how much I missed it."

"You could reacquaint yourself with it now." It's shameless. I don't even care. In fact, I think I've won when he traces the outline of my mouth with a calloused fingertip.

"Don't worry," he murmurs, the eyes I love burning with arousal and cockiness. "I will fuck every inch of this. And you."

He hauls himself out of the water, leaving me gawking at his dripping body.

I'm already thinking about begging him to come back and finish what we started when the phone alarm goes off.

4

Annie

s I slide out of the car, I stare at the text I fired off to my stepmom on the way to the club.

Annie: Tyler and Dad are buying Wicked? WTF???

Deciding it's a little harsh, I add one more.

Annie: Safe travels from Dallas tomorrow. Can't wait to see you all.

. . .

I pocket the phone and trip into the back entrance of BLUE, shoving aside the million questions that feel as if they can't wait until Haley and my dad arrive tomorrow.

I come face-to-face with a shark.

It takes a moment to realize it's mounted on the wall.

"Watch out, Manatee," comes a familiar voice from the dark hallway to the left. "It's gonna eat you."

I turn to see one of my favorite people.

Beck looks effortlessly at ease in a button-down shirt that clings to his body, shoulders and chest made more defined from workouts with his Hollywood trainer for his new TV show. His dark hair and lean, smiling face are the same.

He holds out his arms, and I dive into them.

"Tell me you haven't turned into a douche since I last saw you," I murmur into his shoulder before pulling back.

"Why would you say that?"

I tap a finger against my lips. "Because your show is number two on the biggest streaming service? But mostly because those are some douchey Prada shades."

He shrugs. "People send me clothes. Legally, I have to wear clothes to go out in public. Win-win."

I grin as I follow him down the hall and into the club.

"This place is incredible," I call, my voice bouncing off the walls designed to optimize sound. "Why did you want to meet here?"

"Free drinks."

I think he's joking.

BLUE is ocean themed—not like a kids' aquarium, but like some yacht fantasy come to life. Rae came down early to check out the setup with the sound engineer, so we decided to have our meeting here because it's closed and private with room to spread out.

"In that case, a soda would be great."

Beck crosses to the bar and talks to the bartender —maybe a little longer than necessary—but when I look, the bartender's the one leaning over the surface, eyes bright with interest.

Rae's already sitting at one of the booths, on the phone. She holds it up, and Elle waves at me from the screen.

"Surprise! Sorry I'm not there in person," Elle says. "I will be in a couple of days."

"Are you kidding? I'm so glad you guys are all coming. We both are," I amend.

Beck pries himself away from the bartender and returns with drinks for us. "Where is Tyler?"

"Working," I tell them, struggling to leave the disbelief out of my voice. "So, what's with the ambush?"

Beck and Rae exchange a look, but it's Beck who speaks. "First, remind me what you guys have planned for the next week."

I shift forward, wary but excited to talk about anything wedding related. "Well, I knew it would be hard for everyone to get the time, given our schedules, so I wanted to make it special. To show everyone how much it means that you're all coming and part of our lives."

I open my list of items on my phone. "Dad and Haley, plus Sophie and Mason, are coming here tomorrow, then we'll all fly from LA together on the charter Wednesday. A few other people, including Pen—who's covering a concert in Tokyo—are coming in later.

"The wedding is Saturday with the rehearsal at sunset on the beach the night before. Thursday and Friday, I have a few things planned... No known allergies? No crazy phobias?"

"No foursomes. It's in my new contract," Beck says, apologetic.

Rae presses her lips together to keep from laughing. "I'm sure Annie will keep that in mind."

"Speaking of wedding events, thanks for not

making us wear matching powder-puff dresses," Elle says.

Beck shakes his head. "I still can't believe you're shunning the time-honored tradition of dressing your friends in shrouds so you look hotter. It's bad karma."

I laugh as he straightens in his seat.

"So listen. I know you said there wasn't going to be a wedding party."

"Right." I didn't want them to have to do any extra work, and it was simpler to organize things myself.

"But"—he spreads his hands—"we're going to have one."

I frown into my drink. "One what?"

"A wedding party." Beck's eyes gleam. "Elle and Rae figured I should tell you, though I wanted to keep it a surprise longer. The day after tomorrow, I'm hosting an epic event for all the people not cool enough to get an invite to the knot-tying."

My pulse picks up. "Beck, we're not having a party this week." I swallow as I think of the logistics —dress fittings, calls with the officiant, packing, and now this business deal of Tyler and my dad's. "Don't get me wrong. It's thoughtful of you. But you don't need to lift a finger."

"Oh." He offers a charming grin. "The fingers have already been lifted."

A man with cables wrapped around one shoulder crosses to our booth, looking apologetic. "Can I get your eyes on something?" he asks Rae.

She hands me the phone with Elle, leaving me with a phone in each hand. Then she shifts out of the booth by standing on the seat and swinging both legs out to drop off the other side.

"I appreciate the thought, but..." I try to think of the best way to say that even though I'm touched, we simply don't have time. "I'm not sure everyone will be able to make a party at the last minute."

He waves. "Everyone already knows except you, Manatee." He cocks his head, glancing back at the walls. "Do sharks eat manatees? Anyway, whatever's on this little list"—he lifts the phone from my hand and surveys it while I stretch across the table, trying to snatch it back—"you're gonna clear it for two nights from now."

"Annie? Take a breath. You're turning purple," Elle advises from the phone. "Now, I have to go if I'm going to see you in person for the party." She blows a kiss and clicks off.

I'm still numb when Rae returns, leaning over the back of the booth.

"We good?" she asks.

"Yes," I say and try to mean it as I shift out of my seat.

Beck stands as well. "Your folks get in tomorrow, right? When was the last time you saw them?"

"This winter," I admit.

"It'll be good to catch up."

"It'll be something," I say, thinking of the text I sent Haley as my stomach knots all over again.

When we reach the door, Beck squeezes my shoulder. "Hey. I know you're a Jamieson by blood. But you know who your real family is, don't you?"

I huff out a breath. "Yeah."

"Fuck anyone who messes with you," he calls after me. "Including Ty. You've got us. Right, Rae?"

"Go Avengers." Her deadpan has my mouth twitching.

"Thank you, guys."

Their love carries me all the way to my car, until I check my phone to find a group text to me, Tyler, and Dad.

Haley: Family meeting tomorrow morning.

5

———

Annie

When Tyler said he was taking me to dinner, I had no idea what to expect—or what to wear. He refused to tell me, and knowing him, it could be a corner table at the hottest place in town or something simple.

I walk downstairs and see him on his phone, pacing in the living room. I take a second to admire him in his navy shirt and dark pants.

He turns, and his entire expression warms as he takes in my gold cocktail dress and heels.

"Yeah. We'll talk later."

The phone disappears into his pocket, and a grin stretches across his face.

"You know the first time I realized how beautiful you are?" he murmurs as I take the final few steps. He rounds the couch to meet me, stopping a foot away. "Your dad and Haley's wedding. I saw you walking down the aisle, and my chest cracked in two. Because I knew I could never be your friend the way I had been, the way I swore to myself and your dad that I would be."

My throat is thick with emotion. "How do you know just what to say to wreck me?"

He brushes a thumb down my cheek. "I don't want to make you weak. I only ever want to make you strong."

As the limo takes us to the restaurant, we catch up on the past few weeks. I talk to him about handing off the show for the next month, how it feels exciting and scary at once. He tells me about his tour, the anticipation and awe of such a huge production and the reluctance of departing.

"I don't like the idea of leaving you again," he says quietly.

"You'll visit me, and I'll visit you. We decided together this time. It's different."

I thread my fingers through his, tilting my face up for a kiss he grants me without hesitation. As the limo pulls up outside the restaurant and we step out, I take in the vintage hotel with delight.

"When we came here before, it was packed," I say as security inconspicuously walks us to the elevator, where we're escorted by a bellman to the top floor. "I'm so glad you got a table."

We step out and take a short hallway with contemporary art on the walls before it opens onto a breathtaking rooftop patio that looks as if it could hold a dozen tables with crisp white tablecloths. But tonight, it features only one.

"I did better than a table. It's all ours," Tyler says.

Awe fills me, stretching my chest like a balloon.

"I was thinking how we were apart on New Year's. You wanted somewhere with a view of the stars." Taking my hand, he leads me to the edge that overlooks the view below. He gestures to the sprawling acres of West Hollywood. "How's this?"

I laugh. "Star-studded."

His grin tells me he's happy that I'm happy. There's no better feeling than seeing this man happy, knowing I had a hand in it.

"It's really beautiful," I say, "but I can't wait to head to the island. Where we can see real stars at night. I want to sit out under them with you."

Our waitress comes over with a bottle of wine.

The label has memories lighting up my brain. "This is what we drank when you followed me to New York."

When the waitress disappears, he lifts his glass. "To us. Then. Now. Always."

The simple toast is perfect, and I clink my rim to his. "Always."

I take a long sip, the red wine thrumming in my veins the second it hits my stomach.

"What're you getting?" I ask him after we glance at the menus.

"Steak. You?"

"A salad. Haley and I are going to see my dress in the morning, and I need to fit into it."

He leans in, his expression filling with blatant interest. "Tell me about this dress."

My lips twitch. "No."

"One hint." His impatient exhale reminds me he's not used to people denying him.

"No hints."

"You'll tell me anything I want when those heels are locked around my waist in a couple of hours."

Heat floods me.

"I guess we'll find out." I pick up my wine again, twirling the stem. "I can't believe Dad and Haley get here tomorrow morning. Or that Sophie's going into first grade next year. I still remember when Haley was pregnant with…"

His gaze drops to my stomach, and I stop mid-sip of wine.

"What?" I ask.

"I keep thinking about what you'll look like when you're pregnant."

The way he says it, warm and sexy, tells me exactly what he thinks I'll look like.

It's something we've talked about but not in a few months.

"My childhood wasn't the greatest, but whose was? You said I needed something bigger than myself to believe in. I didn't understand it at the time, but I do now." His gaze searches mine, and the hope I see affects me every bit as much as his words.

"You told me once you want children who glare at us with my eyes and scream at us with your mouth." My heart is kicking so hard it might escape my ribs.

"I'll be a musician forever, Annie. We both will because it's in us. But I don't need to have a career like your dad, selling out stadiums for over a decade. I get why he did it though. For you.

"That's why I want to do this deal. Artists flame out all the time, and the next person to burn out could be me. Your dad is the exception, not the rule. This label, run right, will provide for us after I stop being on stage. If you ever decide to stop, for kids or any other reason, you won't have to worry. Nor will our kids, or their kids, or their kids' kids."

His commitment makes my heart ache. He grew

up with nothing, and I know how important security has always been to him. There's no amount of money in the world that would shake loose that fear in him.

"If it's only an investment, why not leave it in the hands of the lawyers and financial managers? You've worked hard for this time off. We both have," I remind him.

Tyler's brows pull together. "I don't think I realized how big an investment it was when I signed on. But once I started looking through the paperwork, I found something I didn't expect. Memories. We met at Wicked. I got to know you there, in Philly all those years ago. It's a piece of our past, and it could be a piece of our future. Only if we want it," he finishes, sensing my uncertainty.

The tiny lights tucked into the trees leave his face mostly in darkness, and I itch to trace my hands over those planes.

It's hard to argue with a sentimental Tyler Adams. There are few things he holds precious, and the idea that he treasures those times when we first hung out... My romantic heart can't find it in me to deny him.

Still, I hate the thought of sharing him this week for a second longer than necessary. I feel as if I've always been forced to share him, and I promised myself now would be different.

"Most women wish their husbands got along better with their in-laws," I say at last. "But you and my dad have this whole other relationship."

He shifts forward, bracing both elbows on the table. "Before I proposed to you in New York, I went to see him."

Surprise works through me. "To ask permission?"

Tyler shakes his head. "To tell him that I respect him and appreciate what he's done for me but that I would choose you. Every time."

My heart melts even before he produces the small purple giftbag he brought with him. "Open it."

I peer inside to see a small, brown box like a takeout container. Unfolding it, I laugh out loud. "Rice Krispies squares? I'm not sure a nice restaurant like this will let you bring your own dessert from some café," I tease.

"They're not from a café. I made them this afternoon."

Pinpricks sting my eyes as I realize while I was with Beck and Rae, Tyler was thinking of me, wanting to make tonight our own brand of perfect.

"I love you," I whisper, and his eyes crinkle at the corners.

"I love you too. But you said you were worried about fitting into your dress," he drawls, mischief on his face as he moves the squares away from me.

I grab his arm before he can. "One won't hurt."

When we finally get back to the house, it's almost eleven.

"Just saw Haley's text," he says as we head into the house and I hit the lights. "Family meeting sounds ominous."

"She's right. We should get everything out in the open before the wedding. But right now..." I turn to step out of my shoes before lifting my face to his. "I want my husband."

Tyler pulls the door closed behind us. "You have him."

His lips claim mine, warm and coaxing. He tastes like wine and a bit like sugar, and all of it blends with the masculinity that's always been him.

I step between his legs, letting him pull me close. His low growl of approval has the hairs lifting on my neck even before he traces a finger down my back above the dress.

My fingers reach for his belt, and this time he doesn't stop me until I work it off. He lifts me and carries me across the living room and up the stairs.

"Pretty sure your contract forbids you from carrying women up stairs," I say, genuine fear in my throat as we ascend even though his strong arms don't shake once.

"You gonna tell on me?" he teases as we reach the top.

He doesn't stop but walks me right into the master bedroom where I brought my suitcases earlier and sets me on the massive bed.

He kneels over me, lifting my hand to press a kiss to the back. "I've been thinking about how I want to do this all month. Take my time with you. Remind you how good we are together." Then he drags my dress up and presses two fingers between my thighs. "But I've spent my life waiting for you. I can't wait anymore."

He strips the dress off me, and I work his clothes off until he's glorious and naked in front of me. A savage god, but one who knows his own weaknesses.

I want to kiss and touch every inch of him. To take him in my mouth until he groans in approval, opens those impossibly dark, familiar eyes to slits from above me, and says I'm it for him.

"Wait." I scramble out from under him to get my birth control pills. "You meant what you said about wanting kids, right?"

"Yes."

He watches, curious, as I hold the half-used package of pills over the garbage.

"Do it." His voice is a rasp.

I let them drop, and the second I do, he's on me.

He drags me to the bed and pins me beneath him. I'm already so turned on before he shifts between my thighs, nudging me wider so he fits at my opening. The feel of him pressing inside is unreal.

I hope I never get used to him.

"New. Every fucking time, you feel new," he murmurs against my hair.

He builds me up, finding a punishing rhythm.

"I'm probably not getting pregnant tonight," I pant.

"Gotta practice like we mean it."

Once we both come, he holds me against him, our hearts racing together, before he goes to the bathroom.

A light comes on—his phone on the table. I reach to flip it over but catch sight of the notifications.

Dozens of notifications. Emails from lawyers.

I feel sick.

Even if he doesn't have to address all of these, the entire world is demanding his attention.

I set the phone back on the nightstand, but the gnawing in my gut hasn't gone away by the time Tyler returns to bed.

"You okay?" he murmurs as he shifts in next to me, sensing my stiffness.

"Yeah." I nod.

He wraps his arm around me and falls asleep.

As much as I want him, there's been distance between us since I arrived. It won't be eliminated tonight.

I reach for my necklace with the promise ring and the rose pendant.

It's not there.

The piece of jewelry I've had since my first summer with Tyler that's been with me even when he wasn't. It gave me hope when I had no reason to hope, and clutching it in my fist has always renewed my faith—in the world and in us.

I run a hand over the bedside table, then check the bathroom.

Without turning on a light, I pull on a robe and head outside to the yard. I had the necklace in the pool.

I'm fifteen minutes into my frantic search when the gate sounds.

Startled, I bolt around the house to find a woman in a blond wig and sunglasses smoking a joint.

"Rae, you scared the shit out of me. How was your set?" I manage once I recover from the surprise.

She pulls off her sunglasses but doesn't answer.

I frown. "That bad?"

"The set was good." Her voice is unusually tight. "Why're you up by yourself?"

"I was looking for my necklace. I must've lost it in the yard today."

She follows me to grab flashlights. We split up in the bushes, her taking one end and me starting at the other.

"Guys are assholes." The night air carries her voice.

I stiffen, not crossing to her because I don't want to shut her down but working my way closer, my hands skimming the grass. "Maybe it would help to talk about it."

"I said I'd play another night, and I will. But whoever owns that place needs a wake-up call."

I've learned pressing with Rae is like pressing against a concrete wall, but I'm concerned. We all have to deal with hurdles working in this industry, some of which range from gray issues to things that would turn your stomach.

"Gotta remind myself if you have your own back, you never need to worry about who else does."

The earnestness from my friend makes my chest twinge.

We find nothing in this half of the yard, and eventually I meet her back at the patio.

Rae nods toward the pool chairs. I kneel down, peering under one chair, then another.

I eventually find the necklace caught in the pool filter, the clasp broken. Somehow, the ring is still on it and the pendant. I dry it on my outfit and fold it in my hand, heaving a sigh of relief.

But when I stroke a finger over the pendant, my stomach sinks.

"It's broken. I've had it for seven years." I fold it in my fist as if I can squeeze it back together. The feel of the broken pieces against my palm has tears stinging the backs of my eyes. "It's not a big deal."

The spark of light behind me has me turning. Rae's parked herself in one of the chairs.

I drop into the other chair, stretching my legs out and surveying the city lights that twinkle like defiant man-made stars.

Rae holds out the joint. "That's why you're still out here. Because it's not a big deal."

I take it, and Rae shifts back, tugging off the wig and unpinning her hair until it falls around her shoulders. We sit there smoking, the cool breeze prickling along my skin.

"It is only a necklace," she says after a minute. "He'd buy you another one in a heartbeat."

I sigh. "I know it's stupid. But it's kind of irreplaceable." The night breeze lifts the hairs on my arms. "You don't think you'll ever meet someone who makes you cry over a necklace?"

Rae lets out a low chuckle before shifting forward to stare at the city.

"No such guy."

6

Tyler

SIX DAYS UNTIL THE WEDDING

It's hollowly familiar, the feeling of being under the cool sheets in silence. The beating of my heart is a quiet reprieve from the world of chaos where people scream my name when I never asked them to, where executives in cars worth more than the house I grew up in want my time.

But for a few months, I grew accustomed to waking up next to the woman I fell for before I knew what love meant.

We went to bed together last night, and the next time I woke, it was still dark and her side was empty. Thankfully, this morning, light is streaming around the edge of the curtains, and I know without looking that I'm not alone.

Annie's on her side, facing me. Her face is relaxed in sleep, her lips parted, her red hair a silky mess strewn across the white pillow. Lashes a few shades darker than her hair kiss her cheeks, the faintest dots of a few freckles from the scant sun in New York across her tiny nose. Her shoulder, bare above the blankets except for a skinny purple strap, rises and falls with her slow breath.

I want this wedding. I want my fiancée in a dress designed to rob me of my soul. Want her swearing herself to me.

But the world has grown bigger since we were teenagers. We've both changed too.

I went from not wanting children to wanting them with her. And it's important for me to provide for them, to be more than my parents were. Pulling in crowds is fleeting, and it's not the life I want to live forever even if I could.

Still, those concerns feel miles away as I skim the back of my hand over that pale shoulder. The callouses on my fingers mean I don't feel her the same, but they're part of me. Part of us.

My palm slips beneath the sheets to find her waist between her panties and tank top, skimming up her ribcage. "Morning, Six."

The words are a whisper across her skin. My hand finds her hip as I brush my lips over her cheek.

She shivers. After a moment's hesitation, she moves closer, not away. My arousal presses against her, and she rubs softly on my shaft.

I brush the hair from her face, dropping kisses along her jaw and her throat while she sighs.

The clock on the nightstand says it's after eight. Normally, she'd have been up long since given she's on New York time.

And that reminds me Jax and Haley will be here soon.

Ignoring that reality, I move over her and slide a finger between her thighs, beneath the panel of her thong that's already damp.

Annie blinks up at me, sleepy. Her breathing goes shallow, as if even half-awake, she knows my touch and what I'm going to do to her, and she spreads her thighs. It's humbling, the way she wants me.

"Don't move," I murmur. "Don't change a damn thing."

I memorize the look of half-woken desire in her eyes before I drag the fabric to the side and sink into her. She's tight and slick. Just like the rest of her, her body is the perfect combination to bring me to my knees.

Her back arches, her nails digging into my forearms. I thrust into her again and again, building a rhythm she chases with her hips in slow, languid moves.

Annie's close—I know from the little sounds I've heard her make in every corner of our New York apartment, once or twice backstage at her show, and everywhere in between.

She comes first. I make sure of it.

I brush my lips across her temple. "Go back to sleep."

I pad to the shower.

We have a big day ahead of us.

I clean up, dress, and head to the gourmet kitchen. While coffee brews, I check in on work things for the tour. There's a gig beneath the gig that no one talks about, and that's what takes the sweat and blood and tears. It's not the thousands of hours slaving for your craft, it's the next thousands traveling, working with studios and venues and marketing, connecting with fans.

I look through some of the merch they studio sent—T-shirts, a tour poster with a rose superimposed on part of the image.

Fans love my tattoos, but they don't know what they're all for. The compass, the ship, the rose. Maybe they can guess. But when anyone asks in interviews, I need to have some privacy.

The vine roses curling down my left hand, for instance. The hand that got fucked up when we were mugged one night in New York. I've made my peace with it. I used to think it was my tour that did that, and in part, it was.

But the tour was only the backdrop for me learning to live with it. She helped me—her presence, her absence. It always comes back to her.

Annie's the rose overtop, bridging the scars.

The one that holds me together.

The doorbell has me jogging to the front door. I open it to reveal Jax Jamieson, irritated half musician and half soccer dad, in jeans and a black T-shirt, baby Mason stirring in the carrier lifted by one tatted arm. His wife capably fixes a stray pigtail on Sophie, a miniature of her mom who nearly reaches Haley's waist now.

"Morning," Haley says cheerfully.

"How was your flight?" I wrap an arm around her, and she returns the hug.

"Charter was bumpy as hell," Jax gripes.

"Sophie's stomach was upset, but we got a cookie when we landed and she's better than ever." Haley shoots her daughter side-eye. "Funny how that works."

I feel Annie's presence behind me before Haley and Jax lift their eyes.

"Hey, kid." Jax's voice is warm and gruff at once.

"Dad."

"The grownups should talk. Let's get the kids inside and the bags upstairs first," Haley suggests.

We take care of that, and Annie fixes coffee for everyone, then we take seats around the living room.

Haley shifts forward to the edge of the couch. "Your dad and I are so happy we can be here with you this week."

"Thanks." Annie sets a mug in front of Haley but holds Jax's away. "You want to tell me when you decided to offer my fiancé a golden investment opportunity the week of our wedding?"

Everyone starts to talk at once.

"How about we take turns?" Haley grabs a tour shirt off the counter. "Whoever's holding the shirt gets to speak." Jax reaches for it, but Haley holds it away. "Annie, you start."

"Okay." My fiancée takes the shirt and folds it neatly in her lap. "When did you ask Tyler to get involved in this deal?"

Jax starts to speak, and Haley clears her throat. "Annie, want to pass the shirt?"

"No. Why didn't you come to me? Why didn't you think of doing this at a time that wasn't my wedding?"

Jax gets another shirt. "You were too busy planning your wedding. The last thing you'd have wanted was shop talk."

"Jax, that defeats the purpose," Haley says, exasperated as she reaches for the shirt and her husband holds it away.

"Labels don't time their sales around weddings, kid. I wish they did."

"But—"

"The company is going into the ground. We have a chance to revive it."

"You have a label!" she exclaims.

"A small one with limitations I ran into pretty damned quick. Space, for one." He turns to his wife, who nods reluctantly. "Can't expand operations if they're gonna eat into my backyard anymore. Wicked is the biggest name in the industry. They've got a reputation—hell, used to even be a good one. And there's a family connection."

Annie looks between us. "So, you needed Tyler's money."

I rise. "I wanted—"

Jax cuts me off. "You don't have a shirt."

"I'm *on* the shirt," I interrupt, exasperated. "The shirt is me."

I turn to Annie. "I wanted to be part of this, Annie. I could've said no. I didn't. It's not your dad's or Haley's fault."

My fiancée's stony silence has Jax jumping in. "The lawyers can handle the heavy lifting. It's just taking a little longer than we thought."

"How long will it take?" she asks tightly.

"Exclusivity lapses Saturday. We can't get a deal locked down by then, everything falls apart."

Annie shifts out of her seat, yanking the T-shirt from Jax's hand. "Believe me. If you and Tyler spend the rehearsal dinner negotiating terms"—her flashing amber eyes pin me next, and dammit if guilt and arousal aren't a better mix of feelings than I ever guessed—"a lot more than this deal is going to fall apart. Understood?"

I nod, and Jax does too.

There's no way I'm letting this deal interfere with the most important day of my life.

Haley glances at the clock. "Annie, don't we have to get to a dress fitting?"

Mason chooses that moment to wake up and cry.

Haley lifts him in her arms and walks toward the bedrooms. "Jax, help me a second."

He follows, and we're alone.

I catch Annie's hand and pull her back until her chest brushes mine. "You know the only thing I care about in this wedding is that it's you and me. If you want me to back out of this deal, I will."

She looks up at me from half-lowered lashes. Her

amber eyes glint, accented by the faintest hint of makeup she wears when she's not on stage. "If you say it's almost done, I believe you. And you better be present because I have surprises in store."

I rake a hand through my hair, emotions fighting in my gut. Hurting the woman I love is the worst. I swore I wouldn't do it again—no matter how good my intentions. "All I want to unwrap is you."

"I want this week to be special, for us and for everyone." I press my lips to her temple, and she relaxes into my hold. "I have to go to this dress fitting."

"I want a picture."

"You get nothing." Annie steps back out of my grip.

"Then I'll come with you. That's what change-rooms are for."

Her low laugh drags up my spine. "Take those capable hands of yours and put them to good use." She sinks her teeth into her bottom lip as she backs toward the doorway. "I meant signing papers."

"Sure you did."

7

Annie

I wouldn't call it a fight, but when we first discussed our wedding plans with Dad and Haley, Dad had some strong opinions on his contribution. In particular, he insisted on paying for the flowers, the reception, and all the décor. It seemed easier to give in.

Plus, seeing his stubbornness directed at supporting us hit me in the feels.

So, Tyler and I paid for the guests' activities, and me...

I bought my dress.

"Are you ready to see the final version?" the designer, a petite woman with short, dark hair, asks when Haley and I arrive for our appointment at the small all-white storefront in Malibu.

"You have no idea," I say.

I've seen photos of it but haven't tried it on since an initial fitting ages ago.

The designer returns with the garment bag and clears space on the rack, hanging what looks like a relatively modest package compared to some of the huge gowns in the store. She unzips it from the top, and my breath catches as the smooth fabric emerges an inch at a time.

"Annie," Haley says quietly, "it's gorgeous."

I step forward, running my hands over the bodice. It's the palest purple, off the shoulder with a deep V in the front. "It's modeled after the dress I bought to wear to prom with Tyler."

"You guys didn't go to prom."

"No, we didn't."

But I'd wanted to. It was that night, that week, that month that everything crystallized for us.

That I knew Tyler and I would never be the same because I was so in love with him.

And because he couldn't deny me either.

"I made some modifications given the fabric and the fact that you'll be wearing it on a beach." The designer pulls the dress out of the bag fully.

My gaze drags to the bottom in surprise as Haley moves closer behind me.

"What do you think?" I ask.

"I think it's stunning and you should try it on."

I strip down behind a curtain and change into the dress before coming back out. I step onto the small dais—unnecessary because my dress doesn't have a train—and turn in front of the gilded mirror. It lifts my breasts, gives me cleavage without looking too crazy, and fits tightly to my stomach and hips before flaring softly below.

My stepmom studies me, thoughtful as ever. With her dark ponytail and simple, stylish clothes, it's easy to imagine she's a friend or a sister rather than the woman who married my dad.

My attention flicks between Haley and the designer. "I just want to stand in it a moment."

The designer's smile relaxes a degree. "Of course."

When she heads toward the back of the boutique, I spin a little circle. The dress follows my turn, clinging to my curves. The spotlights overhead and the natural light from the front window make it even more ethereal.

"I used to think brides were crazy for wanting everything to be perfect," I tell Haley. "Nothing in our lives has been perfect so far." Emotions swell in my chest, making me clench my fists. "But that's why I *need* it to be perfect. I've been planning this for months, even little details I haven't told him, because

I want this for Tyler. It's my gift to him. My commitment to us."

Her lips purse. "And this Wicked offer makes it harder."

"I hate it. I wish Dad told me before he asked Tyler. Not that he would've asked permission, because Dad doesn't ask anyone before doing anything." I snort as I hold up pieces of my hair, imagining how it will look pinned up. "I know they have their own relationship, but it's like whenever I think Tyler and I have a chance to catch our breath, something else comes up." I shake my head. "I've been focusing on us having this time together. Every decision I've made for the past six months has been for that. I thought Tyler would do the same. That he wanted it as much as I did."

My chest tightens in a way that has nothing to do with the dress.

Haley comes up behind me and squeezes my shoulders. "He does want it, Annie. I can see it in the way he looks at you. But fame is a strange thing. It doesn't wait until you're ready. God knows your dad wasn't ready for it when he was swept up as a teenager. We're rarely prepared for the things life throws our way. Tyler's opportunities are suddenly on a huge scale. He's one man, and he's growing into something bigger than humans were made to be."

I sigh. "I love everything success has brought him. And it's not that I envy him what he's achieved—I'm so proud of him. But I wish he would've included me so we could figure it out together."

"There's one thing I know with Tyler—he's not careless with anything, least of all with you. If he's kept you out of something, he's considered it. Agonized over it. For better or for worse."

Haley doesn't talk much about her relationship with my dad or insert herself in mine with Tyler, but I respect her. She knows what it's like to be caught in the middle of this surreal life.

"You know," she goes on, "when your dad was starting his label, I was pregnant with Mason. He was supposed to do a promotional thing in LA. It was important and had been scheduled ages ahead of time. I called him and told him to come back."

I blink in surprise. "I can't picture you doing that."

"I thought I was okay without him, but I wasn't. So, I told him," she says. "He dropped everything and came back for us."

I turn that over. Even though he's working on other things, I know he'd drop them if I truly asked him to.

But Haley's right that Tyler's growing and he has to deal with new opportunities. I've seen that growth in him even in the past year, when he's matured as an artist, a friend, a partner.

And I don't want the first act of our marriage to be me holding him back from becoming the man he's meant to be.

8

Annie

"What do you mean he's not coming?" I ask in the car on the way back from running errands after my dress appointment. "We've been confirmed for a month!"

"Mr. King is sincerely apologetic," comes the crisp British voice over the line. "I assure you he's made multiple attempts to reconcile his schedule, but running a conglomerate of companies leaves little time for personal commitments."

Disappointment overwhelms me as I scroll through the email correspondence, most signed by an executive assistant at Echo Entertainment on behalf of the CEO. I've been trying to get Harrison King, one of Tyler's friends from touring, to the wedding without him knowing.

I know how hard it is to get on the schedule of a man running a multinational conglomerate, but I figured we'd navigated all the hurdles already.

Now it might be over before it's begun.

When I arrive at the house, the garage door's open. The motorcycle sits out front, and my body twitches the second I see it.

We still haven't been on it. I want to get on the back with Tyler and disappear. But we can't. At least not yet.

Dad and Haley are talking in the kitchen, getting Mason to eat some kind of solids by the sounds of it.

I follow the sound of music upstairs. I peer in the first of the guest bedrooms.

The first thing I notice are the organized piles of merch.

Next, I see my fiancé, patiently holding the strings on his guitar while Sophie picks with an awkward enthusiasm that melts my heart.

The piles dwarf him.

Haley's words come back to me, and compassion and love for the boy who changed my world, the man who owns my heart.

I pick up a Sharpie. "Can I get an autograph?"

Tyler looks up, his eyes brightening when he spots me. "Play your cards right."

"Oh, I'm sorry. I meant her," I say, gesturing toward Sophie.

My little sister giggles in delight, abandoning the instrument to fill the Post-it I hold out with a careful scrawl.

"Do you want a selfie?" she asks solemnly.

"Um. Sure. But I left my phone downstairs."

"I'll get it!" Sophie bounds toward the door and down the hall, and I turn back to Tyler with a grin.

"You have to sign all this?"

"Was supposed to be before we leave for the wedding. My hand cramped up an hour ago."

I survey the room. "I'm tempted to pack half of it up and send it back to Zeke with a note saying, 'Sign it your damn self.'"

"Yeah, but I remember the first concert I got into as a kid. It took months of fixing bikes to earn the money, and I had to hitchhike to get there. A lot of this is for charity, and some of it's for fans who work like I worked to see that first concert. I'm one of the lucky ones, Annie. Anything I can do to give back I'm going to."

My heart kicks in my chest. "You're the best guy, Tyler Adams."

"Maybe not the best. I would like to see you take on Zeke for me. You're sexy when you're pissed."

"Just not when I'm pissed at you."

"You're sexy then too." He winks as he straightens and sets the guitar back on its stand. "You get everything done that you needed to? Remember, I'm supposed to do the anthem at the Lakers game tonight. We have a box so we can bring your dad and Haley and the kids, and Beck and Rae said they'd show."

"Absolutely. It'll be fun. Go team." I pull my imaginary pompoms into my chest before planting a hand on my hip. "Would I make a good Laker girl?"

He crosses to me, eyes darkening. "Fuck that. You're my girl." He drops his lips to my neck. "And you need to take off that skirt."

Electricity jolts through me at the heat in his voice. "Sophie will be back any second. Besides, I thought we had to go to the game?"

"We do. And to get there, I need you to change."

***

When we arrive and Tyler cuts the engine outside the VIP entrance, I laugh, exhilarated.

"I was eyeing this on the way in earlier," I say, pulling off my helmet.

He does the same, hooking his helmet to the back of the bike and taking mine. "I've been wanting a chance to take you out on it too. It's unbelievable."

I feather my hands through his hair from behind. "One complaint. How come my hair's plastered to my head and you just look sexier?"

"It's my curse."

Before I can swing my leg off the bike, he reaches back and grabs me. Tyler shifts me around so I'm in front of him, straddling him. I'm breathless. My legs wrap around his waist as a bead of sweat runs down my back under the leather jacket.

I grin as his lips descend to claim mine.

We're in the middle of a secured back parking lot, the loading docks surrounded by eighteen-wheel trucks and buses, the smell of fumes and asphalt in the air. None of it matters when Tyler's hands dig into my ass. He rocks my hips against his, matching the slow pace of his lips and tongue, content to do slow and maximum damage to my defenses.

"Mr. Adams!"

We turn to see a staff member in black waving from a nearby door.

The second Tyler pulls back, I want to close the distance between us again. His expression says he wants that too.

I shift off the bike, and he takes my hand as we head toward the door. "I'm so ready to get to this island," he says. "Let's skip the wedding and get right to the honeymoon. Leave a note and some food for our friends. They can split the cake however they want."

I pull up, forcing him to turn back, his head cocked in mock expectancy.

"Hell. No."

He musses my hair and has me ducking away, laughing under the watchful eye of the staff person who greets us at the door. We head inside, escorted through the back hallways of the Staples Center, and I broach a topic that's been plaguing me all day.

"I was thinking how good it'll be to have our friends in one place. Most of them, anyway. It's too bad Harrison King couldn't make it. Is there a reason you didn't invite him to the wedding?" I ask under my breath as we head through the building.

"I didn't think he'd be able to come. He's been in a dark place. But it would've been good to see him." Tyler's face goes serious. "He saved my life."

Surprise grips me. "Please tell me you're being poetic. You never told me you were in danger on tour."

Tyler brushes a thumb over my lips. "I'll tell you about it someday."

I exhale a shivering breath. "So, you're what, blood brothers?"

"Pretty much."

I think he's joking, but still... I didn't realize it went so deep.

Security takes Tyler to get ready and shows me a different way to the booth. Through the open doorway, I hear Beck's laughter and see Sophie's head bobbing as she dances in the middle of the floor.

I thank my escort and linger in the hall, pulling out my phone. "I apologize for calling so late, but it's urgent."

The same man I spoke to earlier sighs.

"My fiancé wants his friend at the wedding, and if I have to fly to London and pack Harrison's bags myself? I will do it."

9

———

Tyler

After I perform the anthem for a sold-out crowd of rowdy playoff Lakers fans, security helps me back up to the box we have for the night. The second I see all the people I care about, I relax a few notches.

I make my way toward the front, where Annie, Rae, Elle, and Beck are sitting, drinks in their hands.

"You were a little flat at the end," Elle says.

I rub a hand through my hair, leaning against the back of Annie's seat. "Blame the sound engineers."

"Never blame the sound engineers," Haley calls from where she's grabbing food.

Beck leans over the front, eagerly scanning the home and visitors' benches.

"You been to a game before, Beck?" I ask.

He snorts. "I've been courtside twice this season. The network started offering me seats, and I accepted."

"Can't remember you watching any sports when we roomed together," I say.

"We didn't have time, hustling it out. I had to be efficient with my sports consumption."

"So, you got off to a lot of jock porn," Rae supplies, and we all laugh.

"What about when you went to school, Haley?" Beck calls. "Who'd you date?"

She joins us, sinking into a seat next to him, her eyes dancing. Even though she's only a decade older than us, I know she's seen a lot. "For a while, I had this guy Dale asking me out. He played at the open mic nights I ran on campus. In fact, he was asking me out right up until I left for Jax's tour the summer after junior year and was ready to pick it up after I got back."

"What happened?" Rae leans across to grab some popcorn from the bin Beck's holding.

"Jax showed up."

Annie's jaw drops. "Dad went to a campus open mic night?"

"He wasn't there for the music," she admits, cutting a look toward her husband.

Jax approaches, looming over us in a dark button-down and jeans. An Astros hat shields his face from any fans looking too closely from nearby seats. "The hell you talking about, Hales?" He folds tatted arms over his chest. "You make it sound as if I chased your ass all over town."

"You chased me over a lot of towns," she replies, deadpan.

We all crack up, except Jax, who's left shaking his head, a look of adoration on his face.

Until he turns to me, motions me aside. "We need to talk."

Annie glances between us, her smile freezing before she returns to her friends, who're talking about Beck's show.

I follow Jax to the bar at the back.

After ordering a bourbon, he says, "We have a problem."

When the bartender nods to me, I shake my head. "I thought we had a revised estimate on the debt. Lawyers said we're in the right ballpark now."

"We are. It's not Wicked. It's the artists. Ones with contracts coming up. They're saying they won't stick around if the company sells."

I frown. "But they're the ones who subsidize the up-and-coming talent."

He nods. "The label won't be solvent if we don't have those existing artists producing hit albums."

The bartender returns with Jax's bourbon, and we step away for some privacy, staring out over our friends who're watching the game.

He's right. Jax has been involved in the music industry for twenty years—since he was still a teenager. He might be judgmental and brusque, but he knows the industry inside and out. He's made his fortune there, and taken his share of beatings there too.

"I know." For once, he's reading my mind. "This is the last thing either of us want to be doing this week. We can offload more to the lawyers—"

"No. If we do this deal, I want to know we're doing it right."

I'm not sacrificing a second of this week for some half-assed attempt.

I watch our friends and family talking and laughing. Nearly all of them have a career in the spotlight, but here, with each other, they can let their guard down.

An idea scratches at the back of my brain. "If the artists are the last hurdle to getting this deal done, we need to get their trust. Show them we have their backs."

"Might work. But we're leaving for an island in a day and a half. Unless…"

I cock my head.

"We invite a few. A show of good faith," Jax says.

"Hell no." The answer is immediate. "We're not inviting them to our wedding, Jax."

"They don't have to come to the wedding. They're not going to show at the ceremony. It's a gesture. Invite them to the island, we spend half a day talking with them. That's it."

Annie comes over. "Enough business. I thought you had good news today."

"We did, but there was a complication," I say, searching her face. "You said a couple of rooms were left in our hotel booking. How many?"

She sends a text to the wedding planner, and a response comes immediately. "We have three."

"We were thinking of inviting a couple of artists from Wicked."

Annie's mouth parts. With each second it takes her to respond, the worry in my gut expands.

"To our wedding?" Her voice is deathly quiet.

Heads turn from the front of the box as if they can sense the intensity shift, and even Jax flinches.

"To the island," I amend. "And only if we have the space. We'd handpick people you're comfortable with, but it would go a long way to show them we look after our own."

My fiancée looks between us as if we've each grown a second head before she returns to Haley and our friends without a word.

Jax claps me on the back. "That went better than I expected."

10

———

Annie

FOUR DAYS UNTIL THE WEDDING

"How many people did Beck invite?" Tyler asks as I shift out of the car.

"Knowing Beck, probably every-one." The music emanating from our friend's house has blood pumping through our veins as Tyler shuts the car door behind me, his smile mysterious as he threads his fingers through mine.

My heels match my silver cocktail dress, a vintage number with mesh lace detailing along the curved neck and hem that hits halfway down my thighs. Tyler looks breathtakingly handsome in a button-down open at the collar and rolled up at the sleeves over dark pants.

There's no point knocking. It's clearly a party from the buzz and the music. But before I can head inside, Tyler holds me back.

His gaze skims over my outfit, lingering on my legs in a way that makes my entire body tingle before coming back to my face. "What I wouldn't give to have you to myself right now."

"A house full of tour merch?"

He grins. "You're funny."

"I try."

When I glance down at our linked hands, my skin is pale against the dark swirls of ink that cover his forearm and every inch of his hand. A little rush runs through me, the same one I feel every time.

"Hey. Where's your rose necklace?" he asks.

I press a hand to my throat. "It didn't really go with this dress."

It's a lie by omission as I think about the broken pieces. But I don't want to say it's broken, as if admitting means there's something broken with us.

I'm trying not to think about agreeing to invite three Wicked artists to our wedding weekend, two of whom I realized I'd met before and one whom Tyler could vouch for. They probably won't even come, but if they do, my fiancé promised it won't take more than a few hours of meetings and will be concluded long before the rehearsal.

All I want to think about is the wedding, but even when Tyler and I fall into bed at night, every second he's not worshipping me, it feels as if part of him is somewhere else.

It's probably in my head, nerves about the wedding, and I'm trying to find justifications for them. I resolve to focus on tonight.

On the other side of the door is a wonderland. It's a beautiful house filled with beautiful people. Beck's friends with everyone, and the man of the hour is holding a captive audience in the cavernous kitchen.

He looks over their heads, flashing the easy grin that's brought men and women to their knees. "You guys are here!"

Beck cuts through the crowd, and every head turns to follow him. He gives us each a one-armed hug, steering us toward the kitchen, where a bartender is hard at work.

"Don't tell me what you want to drink. I had this made for you." Beck gestures to a bottle of champagne, and Tyler and I exchange a look. "It was a joke! Fuck, you guys. I know you hate bubbles." He nods to the bartender. "But top me up."

Tyler gets a soda while I ask for white wine.

I recognize Elle in a black dress, her blond hair in

waves that end right below her jawline. Her face is split into a wry grin at something another partier said as I rush to embrace her.

Dad and Haley are on the other side of the doors open to the patio walled in by high trees for privacy.

Beck takes us outside to low lounge couches surrounding a coffee table with a fire in the middle. My arms prickle from the contrast between the cool evening air and the heat.

"You know everyone, right?" Beck asks casually, pointing out person after person he works with.

"Oh, one more introduction. Incoming."

I look up from my phone in time to see a furry shape bounding toward me. At the last minute, it heads for Tyler instead, humping his pant leg.

My jaw drops. "You got a dog?!"

"Fostering," Beck corrects. "And my new roommate here has issues with my former roommate." Beck cackles. "Down, Ernie," he says, mock sternly.

I stroke the furry creature, a black mop that comes to my knees. "Ernie?"

"Named for Ernest Hemingway," Beck confirms. "A man's man."

I laugh as the dog amps up its attempts at my fiancé.

"At least he has good taste," I comment, and Tyler shoots me a pained look.

Out of nowhere, the bartender cuts through the crowd with a tray of shots glowing dully emerald in the light.

"It's a little late for juicing," Elle chides, but Beck ignores her and goes to stand on the back of the couch like some emerging A-list god.

"Hollywood has a rule. Keep your friends close and your enemies closer."

There's no glass-clinking or throat-clearing required for his smooth, warm voice to carry over the chatter. Every head turns toward him, every conversation dying under the force of his magnetism.

"I say who needs friends when you have rivals? People who keep you sharp and have your back at once."

I look around, the faces familiar in the dark, and my chest tightens in gratitude.

"Each person here wants something and wants it bad enough to put everything on the line." Beck gestures to the valley below. "Every light you see is a dream. We all have them, and we come here until they go out or they come true."

Tyler stands tall next to me in the dark, his presence warm and sure.

"It's easy to feel alone, but if you find people to dream with and still make it on your own?" He shakes his head. "That's something fucking special.

So, congrats to my favorite friends and eternal rivals." Beck lifts his shot. "May the light of your dreams always shine together."

The scene surrounding me blurs, and I swallow, lifting my drink. Next to me, Tyler does the same. We all toss back the shot together, and the green drink tastes tart on my tongue before the alcohol seeps in, warmth spreading through my stomach and chest, leaving my arms tingling.

Beck drops off the couch and we hug him.

"Thank you," I murmur.

Motion by the front door catches my eye, and I wave Rae over.

Elle approaches too, and Beck wraps an arm around her neck and takes in the five of us.

"You ever think we'd be here?" she asks.

Tyler's a massive success. Elle and Rae are both hustling it out and doing well enough to land jobs across the country. I've produced and starred in a show running on Broadway. Beck has a hit TV show.

"Fuck yeah," Beck says. "How was I supposed to pay for this house?"

Elle snorts. "How *are* you paying for this house? You got enough for season two of your show?"

"And I'm pitching a reality show. *Being Beck.*"

Rae shakes her head. "You couldn't pay me

enough to have people follow me around with cameras."

"That's because you don't like the spotlight." Beck says it fondly, and Rae lifts her glass, her bracelets shifting up her wrists.

Underneath are dark marks that have me frowning.

I pull Rae aside. "Did something happen to you?"

Her dark-lined eyes don't flicker. "I'm taking care of it. The one place I'm untouchable is in the booth. Someone thinks they can touch me there? They're gonna have a problem."

Protectiveness rises up, and I vow to follow up with her later, away from prying eyes.

People come over and congratulate us, wave after wave. Some of them want to talk about the wedding, but most want to know about Tyler's tour.

I wind my way into the kitchen, fielding congratulations with every step, and order water from the bartender.

A man already at the bar turns to take me in. "Congratulations, Annie."

"Zeke," I say in surprise. "I didn't realize you were here."

The exec responsible for Tyler's big break leans in to air kiss both my cheeks.

"How could I miss celebrating my favorite

talent?" he says when he pulls back. "I've barely seen Tyler at the label the past two weeks. I was starting to wonder if getting married meant we'd never see him again."

Zeke's always been out to control Tyler. Now that he's a star in his own right, Tyler's bought himself some breathing room, allowing him to record with my dad and in New York. Returning to LA this past month was a compromise.

"If you don't see him again, it'll be your fault, not mine. He's drowning in enough merch to sink a warship."

"There's more coming."

"There better not be. He's been working nonstop. It's going to be busy with the tour, and that was before he and Dad started on..." I trail off as I realize my mistake, but Zeke's hand tightens on his drink.

"Working on what?"

"Nothing."

He tosses back the last of his drink, eyes narrowing on me. "There are rumors swirling about a shake-up in the industry. You wouldn't know anything about that, would you?"

Dammit.

I force a bland smile. "I do eight shows a week on Broadway. I can barely keep up with my own job."

I can't find Tyler.

I've been telling myself everything will be fine after my conversation with Zeke, but the nerves won't go away.

At first, I was drawn into conversations with friends and strangers as Beck introduced me around, deciding I should screen-test for his show. Now I wander through the house, looking for the bathroom.

One door I find is closed with a light under it. There must be another on this floor.

On the other side of the kitchen and down a hall, I spot a second closed door. A yapping at my feet has me looking down to find Ernie, who paws at the door.

"What's wrong?" I ask, bending to pat him, hoping his smooth fur will ease the knot in my stomach. It doesn't. "Where's Beck?"

He trots off with a sigh, and I straighten, reaching for the handle and turning it slowly.

I pull it open to reveal a surprisingly occupied coat closet.

"Tyler?!"

"Shut the door." He reaches past me to do it for me, pulling me into the closet with him and drowning us in darkness except for the light from his phone screen.

He's hunched so his head doesn't hit the bar in the middle, and I have to duck a little in my heels too.

"Wait for it," he says, his face still handsome in the ghostly light.

Then the dog is back, scratching at the door.

My lips twitch. "You're hiding from Ernie?"

"Not hiding. Avoiding." But Tyler smiles too, and the tightness in my stomach eases. I can't help laughing, and he leans in, resting his forehead against mine. "It's not that funny."

"Yeah, it is."

We're close, our breaths mingling in the tiny closet. Tyler looms over me, his strong body filling the width of the space, his subtle scent flooding my nostrils.

"How are you enjoying the party?"

"I hate it," he says under his breath.

My mouth parts in surprise. "Beck did a great job."

"I don't want Beck and our friends right now." He threads his tattoo-covered hand through my hair, and I swallow.

"I thought you wanted three musicians from your

future label." Even though we agreed to invite them, I can't resist prodding him.

Tyler shifts closer, and my heart picks up as it always does when he's near me, as if there's no other option but to sync up with his rhythm.

Our rhythm.

"Does it feel like I want them?" He presses my hand against the ridge in his pants, and I suck in a startled breath.

I meant to tell him what happened with Zeke, but I don't want to worry him. Plus, in Tyler's presence, everything beyond that door melts away.

The distance between us narrows as he bends closer, my pulse skittering.

"If you haven't noticed," I toss back in a whisper, "we're in a—"

He cuts off the word "closet" with his firm lips.

His kiss is claiming, and I grab his shoulders for balance as he presses me back against the end of the closet. The phone falls to the floor, the light extinguishing and leaving us in blackness. Coats and fabric tangle around me, and he shoves at them, impatient.

Since I returned to LA, the sex has been insane, but I'm still hungry for more. The scorching physical connection isn't enough to fill the emotional ache inside me. I need the kind of closeness we've always had, the kind that's eluding us now.

He tears his mouth away from mine and leaves me gasping.

"Someone could walk in," I pant.

His answer is to drag his teeth down my neck, making me moan and arch toward him for more.

He's always been the reasonable one. Now he's not.

Those hands stroke up my legs, making me wet from his confident touch even before they plunge beneath my lace panties.

"Fucking need you," he rasps against my ear before pressing two fingers where I'm wettest.

Blind, I reach for his abs, running my hands up his beautiful chest through the shirt.

Every sensation is amplified in the dark, our need turned into a fine point of desperation.

My hands reach for his belt, stroking the hard ridge of him beneath. He grinds against my hand, rubbing against my fingers.

I try to step back and trip on something. Tyler's there to hold me up, grabbing me before I fall.

If I ever thought it would be possible to get tired of him, I was wrong. His passion changes with his mood, with the day, with the weather.

His fingers work inside me, stroking a spot that makes me hiccup breaths against his mouth.

I reach for his belt, but his free hand drags my hand over my head, slamming my wrist against the wall and pinning me with his body. He withdraws, and I could moan in complaint, but he hitches my skirt up my hips, the delicate fabric threatening to tear.

This is vintage. I think it but don't say it, because what's between us is old and new and priceless.

My thong is pushed aside, and he's between my hips, rubbing where I'm slick.

Jesus, Tyler. He's a fire, consuming me, and I can't see through the flames. I want them to engulf me.

I get my arms free and wrap them around his neck, dragging his mouth back to mine. Pinned between him and the wall, I lift my other leg too, and he lifts me higher so he can rub against me, tantalizing and teasing.

Our shared exhale is need and frustration, our lips bumping and sliding.

Until he drops to his knees and I stop breathing.

I feel his eyes on me in the dark. I can't see him, or me, or the contents of this closet, but I sense him.

The second his tongue finds me, I die.

"Tyler."

His groan against my slickness makes me tremble —with strength and vulnerability.

"You." His whispered word is a curse, a prayer.

Tyler licks a trail where I'm burning up for him. Again. This time lingering on the tight bud of feeling at the top.

I grab past his hair for the railing to get more leverage. Every breath I suck in has my ribs fighting with the tight beaded fabric of my dress. It's a beautiful cage.

This man knows how to make me scream. And from the way he's devouring me, he's dead set on making me do it.

"Again." He's reading my mind, and I can't even resent it.

His name is a tortured whisper on my lips, and I feel his response in the way his fingers dig into my trembling thighs, the way his mouth vibrates as he groans against my skin.

Tyler's head between my thighs, worshipping and demanding at once. I hear what he's doing to me not only in my sounds, but my body's sounds. I can hear from the wetness how much I want this, how much he knows it.

My body bends toward him, responding like one of the instruments he's charmed over the years. He builds me up until every inhale is a shallow rasp, every exhale a shuddering sigh.

"Come on, Six. Tell me how much you missed me." He adds another finger, stretching me to the point of discomfort.

But it's the meaning of it that's so sexy I can't bear it—that I'm his like he's mine—and the man I love is just desperate enough to need to prove it to us both.

I come like that, in a moaning pile of limbs and pulsing need. He sucks on my skin, stroking the spot deep inside that makes me shudder. I fall, my head hitting the wall.

Something crashes down on him.

"Did you hear something?" Beck's voice calls outside.

No. No, fucking no.

I'm tugging down my dress before the door opens.

"There you are." Beck looks between us, taking in us and the fallen closet railing. He claps Tyler on the back. "Bar in the bedroom closet's sturdier. All you had to do was ask."

But as he shuts the door, I spot Zeke in the kitchen and my nerves return.

I pray that misstep won't come back to haunt me or Tyler.

11

Tyler

THREE DAYS UNTIL THE WEDDING

"You have to sign all this?" Beck asks, surveying the stacks of VIP fan gear already loaded onto the charter plane when we get to the top of the steps.

"Yeah." I glance at Annie, who's taken a seat with Rae and Elle up front.

Haley sits with Sophie while Jax works on getting Mason to sleep.

"I'll do it for you." Beck walks with his dog, who looks longingly at my jeans through the bars of his carrier as though he'd like to defile them, toward two seats facing one another near the back.

"Doesn't work that way, man." I follow, dropping into one leather seat.

"How long is this flight?" he asks, claiming the other seat.

"Long." I peer out the window at the sunny day. With luck, our destination will be as beautiful.

"Roger that." Beck reaches into the pocket of his designer denim and produces a black eye mask.

"Getting your beauty sleep?"

"In case I need it. We're partying once we get there, I assume."

"Annie has the details planned. She's actually been amazing," I admit, casting a look over my shoulder at the front of the plane as I think of all the details she's taken care of.

I'll make it up to her.

But for now, I rise to grab a stack of tour shirts and one of the four dozen Sharpie markers included with the gear.

The plane takes off, and I spread the shirts—laid flat to make it faster for me to sign them—on the table between us.

"Album's done. You need to take it easy."

"As if you do." I laugh between signatures. "You're filming sixteen-hour days. Plus, I'm not forgetting I wouldn't have my career if you hadn't filmed me playing after Annie went to LA with Finn back in school."

"Make sure you don't." Beck folds his arms over his chest. "What's eating you, T? It's more than this tour."

I hesitate only a second because Beck's the closest thing I have to a best friend besides Annie, and I want to get this off my chest.

"I told you Jax was working on a deal to buy Wicked. Well, he asked me to be on it too," I say under my breath.

Beck flicks a glance past me—a cursory look toward the front of the plane and its occupants—before coming back. "No shit. Why? Besides the cool factor of owning the most badass label of all time."

"It's a good investment for a couple of guys who know the industry. Plus, it means something to me. I want to make a difference in the lives of the young artists there. Annie has her show, and I have my albums, but this is bigger. We're just artists, but a label like Wicked?" I shake my head. "Wicked *is* music, Beck. I grew up at that label. Fuck, Annie and I met there. It's different for Jax—more like a point of pride to turn it around, to fix what's broken because he can. But I want our kids to see it. To have it be part of their lives. Hell, maybe they won't even be into music. Maybe they'll just need college paid for. But sometimes an opportunity comes up when you least expect it, and I never want to be too busy signing T-shirts of my face to notice."

Once we reach altitude, an attendant comes around to give us drinks, and Beck opens the door of the carrier to reassure Ernie everyone's cool. Needing a break for my cramped hand, I shift back in my seat.

"Never saw this happening," Beck muses, staring out the window.

"Us all having careers? You said the opposite the other night."

"That's not what I mean. Figured we'd all be one big happy family. Now you two are branching off..." He rubs a hand over his jaw. "We need to stick together, man."

I frown. "We will." When he doesn't respond, I kick his shin with the toe of my sneaker. "Beck. Come on."

"Teamwork makes the dream work. I know Manatee's my girl too, but it feels as if people are gonna start settling down."

I take back the stack of shirts and grab another. "This look like settling down?" I hold up a shirt with my album cover on it, the tour dates listed on the back.

He chuckles. "Not yet."

What I don't say is that I'm longing to. Part of me

never wanted fame. I love my music and everything it's brought me, but I'm looking forward to a manageable pace.

Annie makes her way from the front of the plane, bending over next to my chair. "Hey. Either of you seen Sophie's board book? I figured it might've slid back here."

I take her hand and press my lips to her palm. "Beck's using it to practice his reading. He'll be at a first-grade level soon."

"You seen T's balls, Manatee? Figured they might be in your pocket."

She grins, and I rub a hand over my face.

"You can stay in the man cave if you want," Beck offers charitably, gesturing to back of the plane. "But you're gonna need to drink hard liquor."

"That's why Ernie's down for the count?" She shoots an emphatic look toward the carrier, and I swallow a laugh. "I'll leave you both with your testosterone," she quips.

We both watch her return to the front.

"I bet you're glad to lock that down." Beck grabs another Sharpie from a cupholder on the table, uncapping it.

"Yeah, I want her to be my wife. More than anything. But she's always been mine, Beck."

"Cocky prick."

"I don't mean it like that. Since I gave her that ring, since the first time I kissed her, since the first time she looked at my blue hair and decided I was worth her time..." I try to put words to the emotions I used to shove down before Annie taught me to open up. "She's part of me. Nothing can ever change that."

Beck draws on a napkin, lines and letters I can't read upside down. "I started pitching this reality series six months ago. No networks were buying because I wasn't a big enough star yet. Fast forward to now, they're returning my calls."

"Your point?"

He pulls back to inspect his work, then holds up the napkin. *Being Beck* is in carefully printed letters with a smiley face.

"Point is, never say never."

When we finally arrive, I'm the first one at the door of the plane.

I signed as many shirts, badges, and posters as I could manage. Now, I stretch out my stiff arms and legs, flexing my hand—even a private plane can't make that long a trip entirely comfortable.

Outside, I'm greeted by sunshine and fresh air. *This will be good.*

I already feel more relaxed. The ride to our resort takes less than ten minutes, all of us piled into cars. Elle, Annie, Beck, Rae, and I share one.

Elle buzzes the window down, taking it all in. "Wow, I can't believe you guys are getting married in—"

Annie covers her friend's mouth with a hand. "Don't jinx it."

Elle rolls her eyes. "We're already here. What could go wrong?"

We get dropped off at the hotel.

"Everything's taken care of," Annie assures us, brushing her hair out of her face as the breeze blows it back into her eyes and sweeps her skirt high up her thighs. I block her body from the wind, and she shoots me a grateful look. "All our bags are being taken to our villas."

She and I have one with a private pool and hot tub. The others have been assigned to either their own villa, or in a few cases—like Rae and Elle—they're sharing. We're staying in a secluded place on the island, and we've been promised there will be little to no intrusion from the outside world.

I don't take privacy for granted anywhere.

"What are we doing this afternoon?" Elle asks.

Annie looks around. "I figured people might

want some time to themselves, so nothing's scheduled until tomorrow."

Rae folds her arms. I don't think she ever sleeps. "I'm going to the pool."

Elle frowns. "I need to bleach my hair before the weekend. I meant to do it sooner but ran out of time."

"I'm sure the salon can do it."

"Nah, it's cool. If I can find an umbrella to sit under, I'll come do it by the pool with you guys."

Beck arrives and wraps an arm around Elle and Annie. "What's going on?"

Rae responds. "Bonding."

He makes a quick count and curses. "Told you, no foursomes. But I should check my contract and see if it stands outside the US."

Annie laughs, and I'm grateful to my friend for helping lighten the mood.

"You guys go ahead. I'm going to see who's checked in," I say, spotting Jax. I need to see if our Wicked guests have arrived.

But Annie jumps in front of me. "I'll stay too."

Despite the long flight, she looks beautiful, but there's an edge of tiredness in her eyes.

"It's fine, Six," I murmur, stepping close and brushing a thumb along her cheek. "Let me do this.

I'll have them send you the list so you can check it later by the pool."

I think she's going to argue, but she relents, her expression filling with gratitude. "Okay. Just give me one second."

She exchanges a few words I can't hear with the wedding planner who came out to greet us, flicking a glance toward me. Then Annie and our friends, plus Haley and the kids, depart in a couple of golf carts. Jax comes up next to me.

Our dedicated on-site planner, a woman in her thirties with shiny dark hair and sun-kissed skin, greets us with a broad smile. "Mr. Adams. Congratulations. We're so pleased to welcome you. We were told to arrange special transport for your excess luggage."

I frown. "Excess?"

"The hold of your plane. There were several extra trunks."

Jax leans his elbows on the desk. "You didn't think what was on the plane was all you had to sign, did you? If Zeke's team is anywhere as enthusiastic as I remember, they packed it full."

My hand flexes, and Jax chuckles, clapping me on the back.

I refocus on the task at hand, turning back to the

planner. "We had three late VIP additions checking in. Have they arrived?"

She consults her list. "Yes, they have. I'll send you their villa numbers so you know where to find them."

Jax and I agreed we'd meet with them officially tomorrow.

My phone buzzes, and I glance at the three villa numbers, a name beside each. "This must be a mistake."

"What?" Jax demands.

The planner frowns and checks her phone. "I'm sorry, Mr. Adams. I was told there was a last-minute switch, but that is the correct name. He checked in with appropriate identification an hour ago."

We picked three artists deliberately—two are Grammy winners, and the third has a social media following in the tens of millions.

But the third person on the rooming list isn't the artist we chose.

Having a plane full of swag is a setback. Doing a deal the week of my wedding is a setback.

This, the name staring at me...

This is a fucking nightmare.

12

Annie

The resort is stunning. A low building we passed on the ride over houses the administration, plus meeting rooms. Surrounding it are lush pockets of trees carved up with pathways leading to the private pods of villas, including the one we rented out for our use.

Nestled amongst the paths are sparkling pools and flower beds exploding with pink and purple and white.

But the island itself is the main attraction. Lush vegetation, palm trees, a balmy breeze that makes me feel as if I'm on another planet. Far from the hustle New York and LA both personify in their own unique ways.

I frown at my phone—no list from the resort or

Tyler yet. I had asked the woman at the desk to keep one detail off the shared rooming list.

My stealth wedding gift to Tyler—one grumpy British billionaire—hasn't checked in yet.

The attendant parks the golf cart in front of our villa, a light sand-colored building, and shows me up the walkway, holding the door.

When I step inside, I suck in a breath.

It's beautiful, wood floors and open air. There's a kitchen and living area that opens to a patio beyond, but I head down the hall to the bedroom. An enormous bed with wooden posts, plus a lounge area on one side with low chairs. The attendant sweeps the doors open to reveal a private patio with a hot tub and its own lap pool.

"It's perfect," I tell him. I can't wait to spend time with Tyler here.

But first, I have something to do.

The attendant departs, and I open my suitcases, pulling out a pink two-piece bathing suit. When Rae said she was going to the pool, I wanted to be there too. We haven't had a moment together alone, and I'm determined to find out what happened at her gig. This whole week is about family and friendship, and what Beck said the other day is right—everyone here with us is as good as family.

Once I've changed into the bathing suit and pulled a wrap overtop, I head out of the villa with a beach bag on my shoulder and aviators on my nose. This part of the resort is private, with a dozen villas surrounding a shared pool. When Tyler and I saw it, we knew it would be perfect for our intimate wedding and for family and friends to spend time together.

I pad across the little walkway to the pool area, spotting Elle already there and pulling a patio umbrella over to her lounger. Beck is dressed in trunks and chatting up the bartender.

"What'll you drink, Manatee?" Beck calls.

I consider as I approach, stopping next to him at the bar shielded by a thatch roof. I tug the sunglasses down my nose to inspect my friend. "Coffee."

He laughs. "Only with a chaser."

He orders me a margarita to go with my coffee, and a few minutes later, both are in front of me courtesy of our personal bartender, plus a margarita for him. We clink mugs and glasses.

"You aren't worried about your abs?" I tease, nodding toward his six-pack stomach.

"My dad might be a prick, but I have exceptional genetics."

"So, you won't be checking out the gym while you're here."

He shakes his head vehemently while he answers, "Every day at 6 a.m."

I throw my head back and laugh before starting back toward the loungers with a coffee in one hand and a margarita in the other.

Beck and I shift into seats next to Elle.

"Your speech at the party was epic," she informs him. "All that stuff about togetherness. You must be practicing for your Emmy acceptance."

"I do have a working draft on me at all times," he says. "But for real, I gotta remind you fools in love there's a more important commitment than to each other."

"Which is?" Elle asks, opening a package of hair dye and laying her supplies out in front of her.

"To the group. We're together for life," he vows.

The words help soothe the dull ache in my stomach, and I lean over and hug Beck. "We're going to remind you of that once you're a legit A-lister and want nothing to do with us."

"Impossible."

Rae comes over wearing a one-piece with denim shorts, and I wave her to the lounger next to me.

"You need a hand with that?" Beck asks Elle, watching her open her bleach and mix it in the shade.

"Nah, I've been doing my roots for ages."

"Without a mirror?" Beck asks. "All right, Annie's not going to say it, so I will. Think of the pictures. I'm not being photographed with a zebra."

Elle rolls her eyes. "Okay, fine. Hold your phone camera up for me?"

Beck turns to do that, and I focus on Rae as she drops onto the next lounger.

"Cute bathing suit."

She grunts as she reaches for sunscreen. She applies it, twisting to reach her back.

"Here, I've got you." I take the tube from her hand and rub some into her skin, scanning for any other marks.

Beck and Elle are talking about some new joke she's working on, and I lower my voice.

"The other night after your set," I say under my breath, "I noticed you had bruises on your wrist. As if someone had put their hands on you."

Rae stiffens but doesn't answer. When I hand the tube back to her, I look at her wrist, still covered in bracelets.

"It happened the first night in LA," she says at last. "The booth at BLUE is in the middle of the bar. Partway through my set, this guy grabbed me from behind. Security was busy doing something else. I told them afterward they needed to pay more fucking attention, and they said they would. But the next night, I saw a woman getting pawed on the dance floor. She motioned for help, but no one came. I ended up leaving the booth and found her huddled in the alley behind the club. Her skirt was ripped. Her fucking hands were cut."

Shock rises up. "That's bullshit."

"It's assault," she corrects. "And they weren't going to do anything about it."

Disbelief and anger clash in my chest.

"I told her to go to the police station to make a statement, even put her in a cab with all the cash I had on me to make sure she got there okay. I don't know if she did. But if the club had done their fucking job, it wouldn't have happened."

"Did you talk to the promoter who booked you?"

"He brushed it off. I'll take it to the owner." Rae shifts back in her chair, sliding her glasses on her face. "But it's part of a corporation and it's hard to find someone to take responsibility."

"Let me help. If anyone puts their hands on you, I will hunt them down myself," I vow. "Which corporation?"

"Echo Entertainment Sont Group. They have clubs from Paris to Ibiza."

Echo Entertainment. My stomach knots, but if I look ill, Rae doesn't notice.

"It's not like I've never been treated like shit as a

woman breaking into music. But when that happens in public and the people whose job it is to have your back turn a blind eye..." She shakes her head. "You hear about the industry, but it's not until you're in it that you experience it firsthand."

"We'll fix this."

Is it just me, or do the words sound hollow?

Because I know the man who runs Echo Entertainment, and he's on his way here.

"Whatever." Rae stands and kicks off her shorts before I can decide what to say. "I'm going swimming."

She heads for the pool steps, and Beck hollers at her, "No. There's only one way to enter a pool, woman."

He rounds to the deep end, his body shining in the sun and his RayBans firmly in place. Standing at the head of the pool, he holds up his arms as if demanding the world bear witness.

"Well?" Elle drawls from where she's reading a book, her roots covered in white goop.

"It's called building suspense," Beck tosses back.

Then he cannonballs into the pool.

There's a huge splash before he strokes down the pool and surfaces in the middle, tossing his hair back. He's carefree, and it's contagious. Still, I can't completely join in because Rae's comment is still echoing in my brain.

"You gonna pull a 'my makeup will get fucked if I dive in'? Because I flew hours from LA to get away from that."

Rae flips him off before jumping into the pool right on top of him.

I have to tell her about Harrison King. But the second I do, all the ease in this moment evaporates. Ease all of us have deserved.

He's not even here yet. There's nothing to do right now, I decide. So, I drain my margarita, leave the coffee, and follow them in.

A few minutes later, Elle's gone somewhere to grab a giant unicorn float and drops into it, bobbing around us while we talk. It feels like school and nothing like it.

Rae looks past me, yanking off her sunglasses. "What the fuck is he doing here?"

I turn, seeing a figure in khakis and a white T-shirt. It takes a moment for recognition to set in, but when it does, I'm floored.

Finn Harvey approaches, one easy step at a time. It's as if no time at all has gone by since he was my mentor at Vanier even though I haven't seen him in more than three years, since I followed him to LA when Tyler and I were struggling and sang backup at a few of his gigs.

He's handsome, and smug, and entirely at home on this island.

I haul myself out of the pool and drip across the patio to where he's standing. "Finn? What are you doing here?"

Finn cocks his head, grinning. "You're the one who invited me. Figured you needed a backup groom or something."

My laugh is loaded with disbelief. "I invited you?"

"All I had to do was get on the plane that picked me up."

I'm beyond confused, but something scratches the back of my brain. "You're one of the artists from Wicked."

His grin widens, accompanied by a slow survey of my body that takes longer than it should. "It's good to see you again, Annie. I've been following your career with more than a little interest. And I like to think I had a hand in it."

I glance over my shoulder to see Rae watching with interest, along with Beck and Elle. Something tells me they would be over here in a second if they thought something was wrong or I was in danger, but Finn and I are just talking.

The bartender appears at our shoulders, offering to bring Finn a drink.

Before I can protest, Finn asks, "What's she having?"

"Coffee and a margarita," the bartender responds.

Finn laughs. "I'll take a vodka on the rocks."

"So, Tyler invited you," I say when the bartender disappears.

"See, that's what's fucked up about this industry. I know more than you do about the guy, and you're marrying him."

The words have me bracing for a fight. "That's not true. He has his career, and I have mine. This week is about me and Tyler making a commitment in front of our family and friends. To each other."

"Then why am I here?"

I pause because I don't know where he fits in. From his raised eyebrow, Finn knows exactly what I'm thinking.

"Let me give you one more piece of advice. A wedding present," he goes on. "Artists are self-centered. They don't commit to another person."

His drink shows up, and he takes a sip before his gaze jerks past me, eyes narrowing on something in the distance.

"Well, this should be interesting."

13

Tyler

It's an unavoidable part of life that other men check out my fiancée.

She's beautiful enough to turn heads on the street, not to mention on stage.

Except when I shift out of my golf cart to see Finn Harvey checking out Annie on the private island where we're getting married, it feels *very* avoidable.

Before I can reach them, Beck shifts in front of me and plants a wet hand on my chest. "Slow your roll, T." His voice, low and deliberate, is more of a warning than the words. "You look as if you want to rip his spine from his body Mortal Kombat-style."

My attention drags slowly to my friend's serious face. "Wanna help me?"

"Hell yeah. But *you* don't want me to help you

because it will undo all the groundwork you've laid, and I assume Finn McDouchebag is one of the artists you and Jax invited here to woo for your deal."

Beck doesn't miss much.

I struggle for control. It's typically my superpower, but as I see Finn talking to her, control slips through my grasp like white sand from the beach behind me.

Because they were in LA together for several shows, while she was angry at me.

"I never thought I'd have to tell you this, but focus, man," Beck reminds me. "You got the girl."

I huff out a breath, conviction settling low in my gut.

I brush past him, pulling up between my fiancée and the man I evidently have to play nice with for the next three days.

"Finn," I say tightly, taking in the man who looks entirely comfortable in a white linen shirt.

The smile he flashes is one the cameras would love, one that would have every social media person coming in their pants and every Instagram advertiser toppling over one another to tie him to their brand.

"The last time I saw you, you were on a stage and she"—he winks at Annie, which I hate—"was following me to LA."

"We all make poor choices in school."

Annie shoots us both a look before turning to leave. "New bikini," she explains. "If there's a pissing contest, I don't want to get caught in the cross-stream."

A laugh that sounds distinctly like Beck's comes from one of the patio chairs.

"You'll make a stunning bride," Finn calls after her.

I wonder if he'd be as relaxed after I shoved his head in the pool.

"Let me guess, the niceties are over?" he tosses, turning back to me with a smug grin.

He's standing between you and getting this deal done. And once you get this deal done... you can enjoy the next month worshipping the woman you love.

"After Shannon Cross died, Wicked fell into the hands of executives who cared more about money than artists. Jax and I have plans to remedy that once our offer is accepted. Young artists are the ultimate future of the company, but you're its present. We can't do it without you." Each word is glass in my mouth.

"This must be a point of pride for the family you're marrying into," Finn says.

"We see an opportunity to help the industry, to save one of the most prominent labels."

"What if it doesn't want saving?"

My arms cross my chest as I try to guess his game. "Then you can go down with the ship. But there are other artists whose careers are only beginning, and I won't let them go without the chances we've both had. Neither you nor anyone else is going to keep me from that."

His eyes flicker, though I can't read the emotion beneath. Eventually, he laughs. "I admire you. If I was set to marry that woman this week"—he looks toward the villa—"I'd have nothing on my mind or my calendar except making her very, very happy."

Every muscle in me clenches.

Finn's gaze drops to my left hand, the one covered in ink, the one that's fucked up. "And it'd be so much easier seeing as how I have two good hands to please a woman."

He doesn't know everything going on, but the comments have my gut twisting sharply, in anger and guilt.

"Ty," Beck calls, his voice a warning. "Let me get you a drink."

"I could use another too," Finn tosses over his shoulder.

When Finn turns back, I'm close to him. He takes a step backward on instinct, eyes widening before he can stop the reaction.

I reach for Finn's shirt with my good hand. "You thirsty? Let me help."

I shove him backward into the pool.

I'm pulling on a fresh shirt for dinner from the ones already hanging in the closet when I hear Annie's yelp from the other room. I sprint out to see her bent double over one of the huge trunks.

"That was not here before," she mutters.

"The staff brought them from the plane. I'll have them moved."

She lifts the lid, revealing more merchandise. "You have to sign *all of it* this week?"

"No," I say firmly. "The label didn't tell me they were sending it. It'll keep."

Annie rounds it and heads for me, still in her white towel, her hair dripping over her shoulders. Her cheeks are flushed from the shower.

Fuck, she's beautiful.

Her lips twitch. "You threw Finn in the pool."

I press a finger to her mouth, wincing. "Please don't say his name right now."

"You invited him."

"I didn't…" I groan because it's still my fault he's here. "I don't know how I ended up with that asshole sharing our island the week of my wedding."

"Easy," she murmurs. "My dad asked you to be part of a deal, and without consulting your *future wife*, you said yes. Through an unfortunate series of events, you invited my ex-mentor to our wedding."

It doesn't feel any better when she says it, and I curse as I pull her hips against mine. "Nothing ever happened between you?"

She arches a brow. "I told you it didn't."

"Tell me again," I whisper. The words are a demand, but my tone is desperate.

"I'm not feeding your ego." But her gaze drops to where my shirt hangs open, and her finger traces the lines of my pecs.

"It's not ego, Six. There's no pride between us."

"Good. What about jealousy?"

Every nerve ending tingles when she touches me, and I lick my lips. "Maybe a little."

She threads her fingers in my hair. "Remember when it was blue?"

I grin. "Yeah."

Annie's shoulders rise, then fall, with a heavy breath. "I liked it blue."

I get the sense she's not only talking about my hair. That she's remembering how things used to be.

Which is its own kind of fucked because they

weren't simpler when we were friends fighting our attraction, our connection. They sure as hell weren't simpler when we were starting a relationship behind her dad's back.

Were they?

"I love you," I say. "More than anything. You know that."

Her tiny hesitation is a blip, the smallest slice of time, but it breaks my chest open.

To cover it up, I drag her against me. My lips claim hers, still warm from her shower and tasting of the sweetness of whatever she drank.

What starts off simple turns into something layered and complete in an instant, like a liquor with a million flavors right beneath the surface.

Annie's gorgeous and raw, kind and edgy, and above all... mine. My best friend, my fiancée, soon my wife.

No matter what Finn says.

I won't lose her. But my grip tightens as if I need to prove it.

"Let's skip dinner," I whisper against her lips.

"But our friends and family..."

"They'll be fine."

She's already pulling back, and I swallow the groan of protest as she glances toward the open doors at the back of the villa. Annie steps away, and

I'd give a million fucking dollars for her to walk back here and let me make her come against the wall.

I want her. Not only physically, but that feels like the easiest starting point to fix whatever's gone wrong between us.

I follow her out onto our private patio. Lush green trees sway in the breeze, and Annie reknots the towel tighter around her breasts as she peers up into them.

"What is it?" I ask.

Little noises come from the trees—peeps and tweets. Annie circles the tree, craning her neck before her eyes go wide with delight.

"Look!" She points.

I stand behind her, following her directions to see a bright-orange bird hiding amongst the leaves.

"Beautiful," she murmurs. "I wonder what kind it is."

I wrap my arms around her from behind. "A cockblocker."

Her laugh tears out of her, and the bird, startled, flies away.

She stares out at the water, the sun hovering over the horizon. "I've never been as excited for a rehearsal as I am for this one. I want to watch the sun go down on the last day before we're married. I want to look at the sky, the stars, for that moment when the world stops and everything is right. And I want to do it with you."

My chest aches. "Sounds like heaven."

If only there wasn't a day of hell between me and that.

14

Tyler

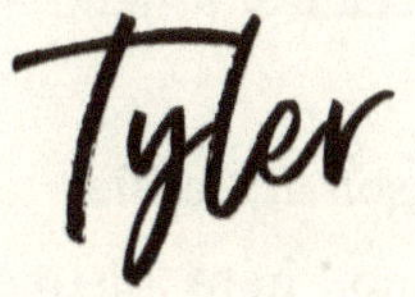

TWO DAYS UNTIL THE WEDDING

"Where's the coffee?" Finn gripes as he drops into a chair across the table.

A moment later, a hotel attendant wheels a cart into the room.

"We all know why you're here," Jax says as Finn nods to the attendant, who fixes his drink. "Tyler and I are part of a consortium looking to purchase Wicked."

"We want to retain the existing slate of talent," I continue, shifting back in my seat to survey the table. "Including you."

In addition to Jax and me, there's Finn and two other artists.

"And you elicit our support through threats and violence," Finn quips, stirring his coffee.

"That was personal." My voice is more composed than yesterday because I need it to be. "This is business."

The other reason it's easier to be composed is because Annie's not here distracting us both by being her.

Which reminds me she and our friends are heading for an adventure across the island today, and Jax and I are the suckers in self-inflicted weekend detention until we can hammer out an arrangement.

I tug on my hair as if that can transport me out of this room.

One of the artists, Den, a strong guy with kind eyes who does mellow R&B music, leans in. "You left Wicked on bad terms after a legal battle, Jax. What makes us think you have the company's best interests at heart?"

Jax rubs a hand over his jaw. He looks as if he could be on stage any second even though he hasn't performed in a few years and is officially retired from that part of his career. "Because I was part of what it used to be. I know it can be better. The music industry is evolving, and we can be on the right side of progress or not."

Flash, a woman with a bleach-blond mohawk and electric blue eyes, frowns. "And you two would be running it?"

I shake my head. "We'd hire a CEO to run the day to day. Any use of company assets by Jax or myself would be contracted separately. Everything would be done above board and ensure there's no conflict of interest."

Finn chuckles. "This whole thing screams conflict of interest. Why should we trust you?"

Jax jumps in. "Let's be clear on what will happen if we don't do this deal. You start over at a new label. Not the end of the world. But without a good offer like ours, Wicked will run out of cash, which means not only will you not get another deal there, you'll have to get in line with other secured creditors to try to get your piece of existing royalties owed to you."

Jax's "bad cop" brashness shuts them up, but instead of confident, they look uneasy.

I study the table. "Finn, here's why you trust it. Because no matter what's between us personally? We're artists too. And we're the best chance you have."

15

Annie

We're all scheduled to meet at the beach at noon, but I'm the first one there except for an attendant who appears to be working on setting up the wooden altar we'll use for our rehearsal tomorrow and the wedding the following day.

I'm distracted by a cage with a bright-orange bird sitting in the sand. The same kind of bird I saw last night from our villa.

"Well, hello," I say, bending to my knees as I come up next to the birdcage. The white sand is smooth against my skin as my jean shorts ride up.

The bird peers back at me, its green head jerking back and forth.

"She's beautiful," I say softly. "What's her name?"

"Hugo," the attendant informs me. "It's a male. The female fruit doves aren't as brightly colored."

"And he's here to get a tan?" I ask with a smile.

"He gets bored up by the buildings. Figured I'd bring him with me for an outing."

"They live around here? I saw one behind my villa."

"All over the island," the man confirms. "This one hurt his wing recently, and we've been keeping him grounded until he heals."

I search his bright feathers for an indication of a disability.

"He's almost right. Another couple of weeks, should be," the attendant says as if reading my mind. "Then he'll go back to his mate. She'll wait for him."

"Of course she will," I say dryly, scanning the length of the beach.

I rise from the sand as Elle, Beck, and Rae arrive. "You guys ready for our adventure? We're going to this secluded cove."

"Hell yes. I'm going to show it to my entire audience," Beck promises.

"No, you're not," Elle retorts.

"Where's our boat?" Rae asks, scanning the horizon.

"Dad and Haley and the kids are taking a boat. Tyler too. We're taking better transportation."

Tyler texted to say they were nearly done and would meet us there. I shelve my feelings about that and look past my friends. I see a string of horses heading up the beach, a rider on the first one only.

"Wild West!" Beck hollers. "I'm so ready for this."

When I arranged this with the wedding planner and the resort, I'd imagined Tyler and me riding off into the sunset. He'd told me he'd never been on a horse before—something about a fear of horses that he promised, after I teased him about it, wasn't really that bad—and I figured it was about time.

It was going to be romantic and cheesy and perfect.

But he's not here. I shove the thought away and resolve to enjoy it until he is.

The trail leader, a woman of middle age with a warm smile and a fastidious eye for her horses and how we engage with them, introduces us to our mounts and tells us the basics. Most of us haven't ridden before, and when I get on, I'm grateful for the saddle to help me keep my balance.

Once we're all on horses—mine is a beautiful black mare named Ilsa—we head in a row...

Out toward the sea.

"Excuse me. Pretty sure these are land animals," Elle calls.

The guide turns in her saddle. "The cove we're

going to requires a bit of off-roading."

She leads us into the shallow water, the horses seemingly content to plod through the water that brushes the bottom of my stirrups. The rhythmic sloshing of the sea against Ilsa's body is strangely comforting.

I sigh in the sunshine, loving the feel of it on my skin, the steady creature beneath me. They carry us around the beach and beyond some rocks.

My mind goes blissfully blank as we round the last shelf of rocks, revealing a new beach. There are stunningly green trees, white sand the length of a football field, birds circling, and craggy rocks at either end.

"It's very challenging to get here except via the water," the guide informs us as our horses plod up onto the beach, stopping next to one another as all of us look around our new surroundings. "The forests are protected, so there's no access by land vehicle from the main resort."

"It's incredible," Elle admits.

My phone rings, and I grab for where it's wedged in my pocket, hoping it's Tyler.

It's not.

"Miss Jamieson," the hotel coordinator chirps over the phone, "Mr. King has arrived. Shall I have him meet you?"

I've been working on this for months, but hearing it's happened just as Rae's horse stops next to mine, the knot in my gut twists tighter. "Yes. Thank you."

Since Rae mentioned the name Echo Entertainment, I've been thinking about it. But she's determined to have it out with the company, and who better than him?

Except this is our wedding weekend. We only have a couple dozen guests, and it took everything I had to get him here in the first place. If Rae confronts him...

Ugh. Each possible outcome is worse than the last. From having two wedding guests at each other's throats to him actually leaving.

We dismount, and the guide sets the horses to graze at the foot of the trees, where little sprouts of grass or other plants are growing. She tells us about the plants and animals here as she unpacks the saddlebags.

"Wait a second—isn't there supposed to be lunch?" Beck asks.

"That will be here with the boat," she tells him.

I look up into the trees, hearing the same birds I heard at our villa.

"Fruit doves?" I ask the guide.

"Very good. His mate could be around here somewhere. Most doves mate for life. They'll always return to one another, year after year."

"That's ineffective. They should have a dove crew," Beck tosses as he heads out toward the water, stripping down to his shorts. "Like a harem."

He wades into the water, digging in the pocket of his shorts.

"What are you doing?" I call after him.

"Filming for my audience." Before he can hold up his phone, he screeches, bending at the waist as if he's been struck. "Something just brushed my leg."

"Sea monster," Rae deadpans. "I read about them in the literature in my room."

Beck narrows his gaze. "Not funny!" But it touches him again, apparently, and he drops his phone. "Fucking hell..."

He drops to his knees, searching in the shallow water until he produces the device. Hitting the power button again and again only makes him bellow in frustration.

The next moment, a sound in the distance has us looking toward a boat coming around the edge of the rocks. The catamaran is sleek, cruising toward shore. On it, I can make out Haley and my dad, plus Sophie's hands waving in the breeze.

And on the back...

The knot in my chest releases.

I get what the birds feel, waiting for their mates. Knowing instinctively it's better to go through hell for the one than try to find another.

My family steps off the boat, wading through the few feet of water to get to shore. Tyler's last, and I take a moment to drink him in.

He's wearing a black T-shirt, exposing the ink that curls down his strong arms and one of his hands. Board shorts cling to his lean hips. His dark hair falls across his face, his eyes squinting in the sun.

He's fucking beautiful.

Especially when his gaze locks on me as he makes it to shore.

"I'm late," he says, stopping in front of me.

"You're here."

Tyler does the same inspection of me, working up my legs under the shorts, my tank top, ending on my face. I reach for the hem of my tank top and strip it over my head to reveal the bathing suit underneath.

My fiancé glances past me at our friends and family greeting and chatting and remarking on the beauty of where we are.

"This my punishment?" Tyler says for my ears only.

"What?"

"You. Looking like this. Especially after spending my morning with a bunch of dudes. Mostly dudes," he amends, reaching for his own shirt.

"How did it go?"

"I think we might have them."

My attention drifts when Tyler tugs his shirt over his head, revealing his gorgeous body. The cut lines of his abs and pecs, his strong shoulders and biceps and forearms.

Groan indeed.

I take Tyler's hand and wink. "I have a good feeling."

He grins, pulling me against him for a hard kiss that has my whole body heated with desire. "So do I, and it has nothing to do with them. I spotted this secluded little cave over there"—he points toward an opening in the rocks near the forest's edge—"that you and I might need to check out." His arms band around my waist. "Clothing optional."

Yes, please.

Over the next couple of hours, we play games, including Sophie's impromptu "What superpower would you pick?"

Beck chooses flying.

Rae chooses invisibility.

Elle chooses seeing everyone naked.

My dad decides on chainsaw arms—so he can

next-level the DIY projects around his house in Dallas. Haley quickly says the ability to heal anyone, shooting Dad a look that has him grinning.

"The ability to be two places at once," Tyler says.

The answer comes so easily I can tell this week is weighing on him no less than it's weighing on me.

After we finish lunch, Tyler and I wander down the beach to inspect seashells washed up on the sand.

"I have something for you." He reaches into his pocket and produces a pink-striped murex, its spines perfectly intact.

I take the tiny masterpiece. "It's beautiful. You found it here?"

He shakes his head. "Earlier this morning on my way to the meeting. I've been carrying it around all day."

My lips curve. "Thanks. I have something for you too."

I nod behind him, and Tyler turns, squinting into the sun as he spots the jet ski roaring toward the shore. "What the hell...?"

Then his jaw goes slack as recognition sets in. "Did you do this?"

I play innocent as I set the shell back on the sand. "It's an early wedding gift. And you better like it because it's too late to send it back."

16

———

Annie

The man on the jet ski carves his way up to the shore, splashing as he goes. An attendant manning the cat takes it from him as Harrison King steps off.

I'm not sure what I was expecting. I knew he was a few years older, but it's extra clear seeing him in person. He's wearing a black short-sleeved shirt, unbuttoned, board shorts underneath. His dirty-blond hair is a mess, his designer sunglasses covering half his sculpted face.

He stalks up the beach with even, purposeful strides and stops in the sand with his bare feet. He tugs off the sunglasses, surveying us with narrowed eyes. Harrison's attention cuts to my fiancé. Then his imperious face breaks into a grin. "There he is."

He crosses to Tyler, clapping him on the back,

and Tyler does the same. "You're here. How the hell did that happen?"

"Someone was persistent." The crisp English accent is one thing, but King looks past my fiancé, his laser eyes finding me.

Tyler introduces me, then I let them catch up as I go over to Rae, who's drawing in the sand with Sophie. They're building what looks like a compound with outbuildings and a moat.

"What is this?" I demand.

"It's Sand City. Less castle, more Coachella. There are ten stages"—Rae gestures to elevated flat platforms—"and a spot for camping."

"And the truck parking is there," Sophie points out.

"Right. That's where you're going to park when you get your license?"

"Yup. Rae's going to teach me to drive."

I notice Harrison watching Rae intently.

"What's his deal?" she asks under her breath.

"Apparently, he had some big breakup and went from being front page of every tabloid and loving it to a near recluse."

She doesn't take her gaze from his. "Girl could do worse than shacking up with that. Long as the place she does it is big enough for him, her, and his ego."

Guilt floods me. I need to tell her the truth: that

Tyler's friend runs the company she wants to hang by the toes.

But Rae finally seems as if she's having a good time, and this would ruin it.

She shoves herself out of her seat, dusting off and heading across to where the drinks are.

"Thank you for coming," I say to Harrison, who approaches but still watches Rae.

"You were obscenely persistent, but I couldn't miss Tyler's wedding. Who's your friend?"

"I don't think she's your type."

He cocks his head, amused. "You'd be surprised how many women are."

"Exactly."

The challenge on his face lingers as Tyler approaches, clapping Harrison on the back.

Harrison turns, starting across the sand to get a drink.

"I don't know how the hell you made this happen. Thank you." Tyler wraps me in a hug, his strong arms every reward I could've wanted.

"You really wanted him here," I say against his bare shoulder.

I wish I could talk to Tyler about Rae's situation, but I'm not going to drop this at his feet when he's grappling with enough already.

He scans the beach behind us before grabbing

my waist and backing me toward the water, an expression of mischief on his face.

"What are you doing?" I ask, already breathless.

He holds a finger to his lips as the water licks at my calves, then thighs, then waist. He tugs me out toward the catamaran and pulls me behind its shadow.

Then he kisses me, hard and deep enough the crystal waters and beautiful surroundings fall away and I'm drowning in *him*—his scent, his touch, his taste.

"There might be sea monsters," I manage when he pulls back, and he snorts.

"I'll protect you."

"I'm serious. Beck already found them," I laugh against his mouth.

"Beck who?"

Tyler's chocolate eyes are almost black, his hair ruffled from the wind, and the turquoise ocean leaves trails of water that drip off his chin and bead deliciously on his shoulders, sparkling over the canvas of black ink that curls around his chest and arm.

He's the most stunning man I've ever seen. And he's mine.

Desire washes over me, through me, becomes part of me like the sea.

His scent is wild and familiar at once, the smoky cedar invading my senses. It steals the part of my brain reminding me we're sharing this beach with a dozen other people.

My fingers tangle in his hair, tugging hard enough he groans. He pulls my hips against his, and the hard ridge of him through the shorts makes me ache.

This week, there've been moments he's felt like a stranger. I feel like a traitor even thinking it when I know deep down he's the Tyler I love. But between a few stolen moments, I've barely seen him.

Now, as if he's thinking the same thing, he drags me back to him.

Nothing will come between us, say his lips, his tongue, his touch.

His fingers skim my ass under the bathing suit, making little shivers electrify me. Underwater, it's even better. His touch is a shimmer, a promise, a tease I couldn't ignore if I wanted to.

"You know what's wrong with spending the afternoon on a deserted beach with your friends and family?" he murmurs against my ear. The friction of his lips leaves me shivering despite the warmth of the water, of his body.

"What?" My arms band around his neck, the buoyancy making it easy to hook my ankles around his waist. I'm reduced to a barnacle on this man, and I don't even care.

"Absolutely fucking nothing as long as we can do this." Tyler's voice is a dark promise before his wicked fingers press where I'm already aching for his touch.

I don't need his satisfied groan to tell me I'm wet. The way those fingers penetrate me, sliding deep, filling me with a confidence bordering on arrogance.

His eyes change color. "Fuck, I've been thinking about this all morning."

My body tightens around him, and one of those sounds rips through my chest, muffled by his shoulder. "Tyler... don't get me wrong, because this is hot —so damn hot..." I pant when his thumb presses against my swollen clit, taking my arousal up another thousand notches. "But I want more than this. It feels like we're stealing moments, and this is supposed to be the time for us."

His jaw works, his nostrils flaring as if he's being punished by some invisible force. "I know. Soon."

His tortured words land on my skin, melt there. Tyler knows it doesn't heal what's between us, and the fact that he doesn't pretend it can makes it impossible to deny him.

Because if all I have with him right now is this

moment at the edge of the world, our life on the other side of this catamaran, I'll take it.

It's never been about sex with Tyler. I'd love him even if we didn't have a connection like this. But our connection leaves nothing untouched. He takes unrivaled satisfaction in claiming me inside and out.

My body, my heart, my soul.

I pull him out of his shorts, and his jaw clenches with need.

"In my mind, we're in a bed," he whispers. "It's you and me and nothing but time."

I shift down onto him, arching my back to take him. "Oh my God." I hiccup a breath, fisting my hand in his hair.

My nails scrape his shoulders, the tattoos across his chest blurring into a haze of black lines as my vision blurs at the feel of him.

"I'm spending seconds as if we're going to live forever. Taking you so slow you swear you're going to come from the waiting alone." He grinds me on him, around him, forcing my body to take him all the way in.

The low rasp of his breathing is unbearably sexy against the background of our friends laughing, the occasional shriek of a bird or of Sophie.

Tyler strokes into me, and I clench around him.

My hands drag greedily up his abs, his pecs, and I lower my mouth to his neck.

He stumbles back until his shoulders hit the anchored boat. "But every time I touch you, every time I give you pleasure, you take a piece of me. And I want to make it last forever because I want you to see it in my eyes every time you do that."

He lifts and lowers me on him, and I ride him as best I can. I rub my aching breasts against his chest. I can't remember the last time I was this horny, but I've barely seen him all week.

It's not enough.

"You feel so good," I mumble against his ear.

He chuckles. "You have no idea."

His hand strokes down my back, grabbing my ass and squeezing. I know exactly what he likes, and he knows me too.

It's what makes this perfect. Worthwhile. No matter what else it going on for us, we'll get through it. I have to trust in that.

As I rake my nails across his shoulders, as his strokes level out from shallow thrusts into long, purposeful motions, we chase each other toward the peak.

My head drops back. Blue sky, birds, ocean breeze.

And Tyler.

I'm there first, my body tightening around him.

"Yes, like that. Come for me," he murmurs.

He's there a moment later, his damp shoulders tight beneath my hands, his beautiful firm mouth parted in the face I alone get to see.

I memorize it, exalt in it. "More."

He obliges, coming for what feels like forever inside me.

He's leaning against the boat, the waves lapping against the side. I'm collapsed on him, my face buried in his shoulder, when noises from the boat above tear into my haze.

"Where are they?" comes a voice from the boat.

Shit.

Footsteps on the deck of the cat echo in my ears as Tyler and I lock gazes.

We spring apart, hoping it's not too late.

If it is...

I will actually die.

Tyler

"We have a problem." Jax frowns as he looks over the side of the deck.

I take in Annie's flushed face. I'm still coming down from the high, and whether or not we look like it, my body is shaking from the release.

A minute later, I'm hoisting myself out of the water and up onto the boat. Annie follows, her suit back in place. I wrap her in a towel before grabbing one myself.

"Don't tell me the artists from this morning have come back to say they won't sign," I say as Jax paces the deck.

"No, they're still debating. But there's another party interested in buying Wicked."

My gut twists.

Jax looks between Annie and me, and Annie lifts her hands. "What exactly is going on?"

Jax grimaces. "I don't want to ruin your day with details."

"You're already in my day. So, you might as well tell me."

He explains that our exclusivity will expire this weekend if we don't get a deal. If that happens, Wicked can try to get another buyer, but there's no guarantee another owner wouldn't focus on proven talent and slash every other cost—including up-and-coming artists.

"Who'd have the resources to bring an offer?" she asks.

"I'm not sure who's spearheading it, but Zeke's involved," Jax said. "I don't know how he heard about this. Everything's under an NDA."

Annie's face goes pale. "He was at Beck's party. I didn't tell him, but... he might have connected the dots."

My stomach drops.

"*Shit.*" Jax rubs a hand over his jaw.

"Don't blame yourself," I say, taking Annie's hands, but Jax's head falls back.

"I don't. You're the one who wanted to buy a

company the week of our wedding." She rounds on her father, tearing her hands from mine. "And you think you can bring your chaos and everyone just rolls with it. I'm not rolling with it."

"Annie—" I reach for her, but she backs away, eyes flashing.

"No. I'm sorry if I made this harder on you by letting something leak at Beck's party. But you put me in a shitty position."

To his credit, Jax looks almost as upset as I feel at the sight of Annie on the verge of angry tears.

She stares woodenly forward for a minute, ignoring both of us, before turning and marching toward the front of the boat, dropping off the side, and swimming toward the shore without a backward glance.

Fuck. I've caused that, and I hate it. I hate her pain. I hate this deal. I hate the guilt roiling in my stomach.

But I'm doing it for us, I remind myself for what feels like the thousandth time.

I love this woman, and the fact that we're wired differently is part of that. She feels everything as if life could be over the next second. I'm the one who thinks about the what-ifs, plans for every scenario from bad to worse. Today, being that person sucks.

Buying Wicked was supposed to do something

meaningful for up-and-coming artists while also providing for the people I love. But as I watch Annie emerge from the water onto the shore to meet our friends, I feel as if both her and the deal are getting further away.

18

Annie

ONE DAY UNTIL THE WEDDING

The knock on my door cuts into the blackness in my room. I shift out of bed, straightening my pajamas.

Tyler's not here.

Worry floods me until I see the sheet of paper on the bed.

Six,

I'm sorry I missed you last night.

We're going back for the final push today.

I can't wait to see you for the rehearsal dinner.

I love you more than anything.

T

The worry is replaced by a dull ache that makes my limbs heavy as I pad toward the door and crack it.

Sunshine streams in, burning my retinas as I squint at the silhouette.

"The wedding planner told me to bring you this." Rae holds out a cup of coffee.

I pull open the door and take it from her, inspecting the label. It says "Bride" with a heart drawn on it.

"She wrote that too," she insists, brushing past me into the suite. "Are you ready for your last day as an unmarried woman?"

"Yes and no." I scrunch up my nose, and she scans the room.

"This is an interesting arrangement."

All the furniture is pushed back against the walls.

"There were a dozen trunks of merch in here Tyler was supposed to sign. He had them moved to some storage place."

"Where is Tyler?"

I rub my face. "I don't know. He didn't come home last night."

Tyler and Dad skipped dinner to work on the deal. But though I waited up until after midnight, my fiancé didn't show.

Regret crawls through my stomach as I think about our fight on the boat.

"Come on." Rae jerks her head toward the door. "We have plans."

I take a sip of the coffee, and the hot brew does something to settle my nerves. "Rae?"

Her dark brows rise.

"What if I was deciding to tell someone I care about some information that they might want? But it might ruin their time off?"

"Normally I'd say tell him. But…" She looks past me toward the open doors, the beautiful morning beyond. I've never seen Rae look so wistful. "I know how hard it is to get a few days off. And most problems will still be there." Her gaze comes back to mine, and she rolls her eyes. "Are you going to go get your ass dressed or what?"

Ten minutes later, Rae and I show up at the day spa in the main building. When I walk inside, there're friendly faces having an argument.

"He'll behave," Beck insists, gesturing to the black puff. "Ernie is all class."

The spa attendant looks at him suspiciously, and the dog barks once as if to emphasize it.

"You made it," Elle calls. "We were getting worried Rae was too rebel to follow simple instructions."

Rae flips her off and crosses to one of the pedicure chairs. She sits gingerly on the edge and inspects the basin below.

I snap my head up when I see Pen walking in, and my jaw drops. "You're here!"

"Of course. I'm not gonna let my best girl get married without me."

I run to her and squeeze her in a hug so hard it's borderline cruel.

"These fools might be famous, but you and me go back."

An attendant clears her throat, and we all turn to look. Four more women appear behind her. She lists off a range of treatments.

"I'd blow someone for a pedicure," Pen says. "These feet have been traipsing through airports all week."

Beck gets a drink and gets Ernie to sit in exchange for the little spa cookies.

"What color would you like?" my spa technician asks, presenting the range of nail polish options. "Something romantic, I assume."

I study the samples. "Do you have something in a

'So Your Fiancé's Buying a Record Company Cobalt'?"

Elle chuckles. "Or 'Guys Leaving You Out Green'?"

The tech looks between us, apparently nervous. "The closest is Forever and Ever Fuchsia."

"Where are the guys today?" Pen asks.

After I decide on a soft shell pink that will go better with my dress than something outrageous, I fill her in.

"So, he didn't come home last night?" she asks.

"He left a note. I get that he wants to help the next generation of artists and he wants to provide for us at the same time. But we're going to be fine. All I need is him."

"He doesn't know everything's going to be fine," Beck points out. "When you guys were mugged in New York and Tyler's hand got fucked... that was hell for him."

"I know it was," I toss back. "I was there."

He shrugs. "But things haven't worked out his whole life, Manatee. You were the first thing that did, and he wants to do right by you."

I submerge my feet in the hot bath, tipping my head back as the competing feelings of appreciation and longing wash over me.

Maybe Beck's right. As maddening as it is right

now, the way Tyler looks out for his own, the way he's become the man who does, is part of what I love about him.

"It can't be that hard to finish this deal," I mutter. "Get the papers signed. Get the artists on board…"

Elle snorts. "Hey, Finn, let me convince you," she says in a sing-song voice.

I throw a face cloth at her, and she catches it before it hits her.

"Wait—what the hell does Finn have to do with this?"

We fill Pen in, and the way her eyes grow with every part of our story is mildly vindicating.

"Enough of this. They're working; we're playing." Beck angles his phone at his face and Ernie.

I cock my head. "Your phone was salvageable after the ocean incident?"

"Nah, I had another one dropped off overnight."

I roll my eyes.

He hits a button. "This is Beck. I'm here with my friends on a secluded island paradise. Guess where?"

Elle dives across the room, tackling him so that his phone flies out of his hands and lands in the foot bath.

"Dammit, E," he complains. "If I'm not in touch with my fans, they're going to worry."

I wiggle my toes as I lift them out of the bath, and my service tech goes to work.

"So, are you excited for the rehearsal tonight?" Pen asks.

Anticipation prickles down my spine. "Hell yes. Want to see the dress?"

I call the wedding planner to see if she can bring it over early.

The silence down the line is horrifying. "I have a note that you were bringing it on the plane with you and would keep it in your villa."

My chest tightens as I look toward Rae and Pen. "I don't have it," I say into the phone. "I thought you were keeping it so Tyler didn't accidentally see it."

"Let's check your villa," Pen says calmly. "It was in a garment bag, so it must be in a closet somewhere."

We head over there in a golf cart, my heart hammering the entire time. We check every closet as acid eats my stomach.

Tears threaten my eyes. "It's not here. It was in a—"

Rae's gaze meets mine. "Trunk. Where did Tyler send the merch trunks?"

We head over to the storage facility on the edge of the resort in our golf cart, meeting the wedding planner outside.

"How much merch did he have?" Pen comments, opening the first trunk to reveal T-shirts.

I don't answer, opening another trunk. Lanyards and VIP badges. We go through ten trunks as panic sets in, gnawing at my insides and corroding any semblance of the cool I've been trying to maintain this entire week.

I stare at Tyler's contact on my phone, needing to hear his voice.

I hit it.

It rings once.

Twice.

Goes to voicemail.

I swallow painfully.

"You guys," Rae calls from under the lid of the final trunk.

We race over to her. Peering over her shoulder, a huge breath whooshes out of me. I squeeze my eyes shut.

"Thank fuck," Pen says.

I lift the heavy garment bag out of the trunk, unzipping it, unsure whether to trust it's here until the zipper parts and reveals the purple fabric.

Pen gasps. "Oh my God. Annie, it's beautiful. Tyler's going to lose his shit."

They help me carry the dress outside, where our

planner is waiting. She promises to keep the dress safe and have it steamed overnight.

I turn to Rae. "Would you keep it for me after it's steamed?"

She blinks. "Yeah. Sure."

When we head back through the main lobby area, I see Hugo in his cage, calling to people who pass through.

"Can he come tonight?" I ask the wedding planner.

If he can't be with his mate yet, maybe he can witness an act of love.

19

Tyler

"Tyler. You still with us?"

I snap my attention to the lawyers on the tablet. "What're we waiting for?"

"They're reviewing your revised terms for the debt restructuring," our lead attorney says.

"Terms which are more than fair," I press. "So, what's to review?"

There's no answer.

I tug on my hair and rise from the chair, the four walls starting to feel like a prison after twelve hours.

I went to our villa to rest for a few hours last night, holding my fiancée while she slept. I don't want to shift the burden of my responsibility onto her, but this situation has tested every ounce of my resolve.

"What if we put this on hold until after the

wedding?" I ask. My fiancée is getting ready for the rehearsal dinner, and I'm in here arguing over technicalities.

"Exclusivity lapses tomorrow. Which means everything we've all been working on for weeks—months—is gone."

I'm typically the cool head in any conversation. Now, I'm frustrated enough to put a fist through the wall.

I hope it's worth it. Annie's words from yesterday come back.

I stretch out my arm, my hand. The place above my knuckle where the ring will rest tomorrow.

Annie and I picked it out together at a jewelry store in New York. Having it on my finger, the weight of it, felt right.

But more than that, I remember her face when she saw it on me. The look of complete and utter devotion. I want to deserve that look. To be the kind of man who takes care of her, not because she needs it, but because I need to do that. To protect her the way I was never protected.

Before I left the villa this morning, I went looking for it in her jewelry box.

I found more than I bargained for.

The necklace she's worn for five years was in a pile on the bottom, the promise ring glinting dully.

The clasp was mangled, the pendant with the purple rose cracked.

Did she break it out of anger after our argument?

The possibility has my hands clenching and my breath going shallow. The feeling rising up isn't disbelief but something like panic.

Annie's always worn her heart on her sleeve. If she's doing shit like that where I can't see it, I've hurt her worse than I thought.

I check the clock on my phone. "There's an hour until the rehearsal. We need to wrap this up. I need to get back to Annie."

Jax rubs his chin. "Haley's not thrilled with me either."

The lawyer smirks. "Women don't understand. Am I right?"

Anger rises in me, but Jax leans in toward the tablet before I can open my mouth. "You've never met my wife, have you?"

His tone is mild. Soft.

Terrifying.

The man on the other end of the call frowns as if trying to remember, then he shakes his head. "I'm afraid I haven't had the pleasure."

Jax leans an elbow on the back of his chair, looking entirely at ease, but his amber eyes smolder. "What about my daughter?"

"Only briefly."

"You think you're hot shit with your Rolexes and your Lambos. I bet you congratulate yourself every night for having 'made it,' for being top in your Ivy League class or whatever gets you off. But you have no idea what it takes to run an empire that wears your face—one that demands and gives in ways you could never expect. Those 'women'? They get it. They live it, and they're the reason we do any of this. Which means they're the reason *you* get paid. So, you can stop pretending you know the first thing about women and stick to what we're paying you for."

Shock, tinged with a little fear, is plain on his face even through the video call. "Understood."

Jax exhales heavily before glancing at me.

I turn back to the screen, blood thrumming in my veins with renewed purpose. "Let's make this happen."

20

Annie

"What's with the mascot?" Beck asks as he makes his way across the beach to where the group of us is gathered.

"He's a friend," I say, nodding to Hugo in his cage, whom the staff let us borrow. He twitters in response.

Beck goes to join the others, but I turn toward the sea. For the rehearsal, it's supposed to be our close friends, plus Haley and Dad and the kids. The officiant doing our service will walk us through. It's going to be short—half an hour—but the importance of it feels much bigger.

I've always loved the sunrise more than the sunset. It's the promise of something new.

But the sunset tonight was supposed to be something to savor—a symbol of the last day of my life alone and a chance for us to watch the stars.

On the beach, the sun glowing like orange and pink embers on the horizon, my simple white linen dress blows in the breeze...

But there's no Tyler in sight.

He'll be here.

The officiant arrives, holding a book under her arm. She smiles. "How are you all today?"

"A couple of bodies short," Elle notes, scanning the row of villas for some sign of movement.

Uncertainty ripples through my stomach. It's almost time to start.

Haley appears around the corner, and the nerves dissipate.

"Are Dad and Tyler on their way?" I ask, my brows tugging together. "They were supposed to be here fifteen minutes ago."

My stepmom stops in front of me, Mason in the stroller. Sophie spots Hugo and makes a beeline for his cage.

"You haven't heard from them?" Haley guesses.

"No." I swallow hard. "We're going to lose the sunset."

The emotions in my stomach are reflected in her eyes. Disappointment, disbelief, anger, grief.

Over my shoulder, the sun seems to sink another

inch closer to the calm sea, and my hope descends with it. *He was supposed to be here.*

Haley squeezes my shoulders, and my throat fills. I knew going in that I was marrying someone whose public star would shine brighter than mine. I even told myself I was okay with it... and I am okay with him being known, recognized, appreciated.

Because he always knows, recognizes, and appreciates me.

"I've been thinking all week about what you said. I've been trying to be mature, to let him take on this responsibility," I murmur to my stepmom, emotion filling my voice.

I don't care about money.

I don't care about the legacy we leave behind.

I need him.

"This isn't about maturity anymore, Annie. Excuse me one minute."

Leaving Mason in the stroller, Haley stomps across the sand toward the villas. Her hair billows in the breeze behind her.

Elle looks dismayed. Pen is pissed. Harrison—standing next to Rae—seems to have a hard time dragging his attention from her while her hands are clutched in fists at her chest, dark expression unreadable.

"I'm going to watch," Beck decides, but Elle grabs the back of his shirt.

"This is a family moment."

"The beatdown of Jax Jamieson? I want to witness, or no one will believe it."

Squawking has me looking over toward Hugo's cage. Sophie's talking to him, and I go over to her.

"He doesn't like it," she informs me, peering up.

"Sometimes you have to do things you don't want to do. It's for the best."

I turn my back as Rae comes up behind me.

"Tell me you didn't know," she says, her voice strangely flat.

I blink. "What are you talking about?"

But her hurt expression has my throat drying even before she says, "Harrison King is the CEO of the company that owns Echo Entertainment."

Breath burns my lungs. "I was planning to tell you."

"When? After the wedding so I didn't make a scene?" Her eyes flash with pain.

"That's not why I didn't..." I trail off. Maybe in part that was why I didn't tell her. "Rae, I'm sorry."

My friend shakes her head. "I know this week hasn't been easy for you, but I thought you had my back."

"What's going on?" Pen demands, crossing to me

as Rae turns and heads away from us and from Harrison.

I curse through my unsteady breathing, hands clenching into fists at my sides. "I wanted this to be perfect. All our family and friends came together from all over the world." Tears slip down my face. "We all hustle our asses off, but I wanted to put it all aside and just be about love. To celebrate how we've all gone through shit but we love each other and we're here. Is that too much to ask?"

A squawking sound at my back has me whirling to see the door to Hugo's cage is open.

The cage is empty.

I gasp. "Sophie, what did you do?"

"He didn't like it in there." Her pout is defensive.

Scanning the sky, I search for any sign of movement against the fading colors. "There he is!"

Hugo's a dozen feet in the air, struggling to fly.

"Probably flying back to the cove," the attendant weighs in. "Where his mate is."

"So, that's good?"

The attendant can't keep the sadness out of her voice. "He's not healed yet. He probably won't survive."

My chest aches as I watch him. I've spent a lot of my life feeling out of control, but I can't come to grips with it right now.

Standing on a beach in a beautiful dress with words in my heart… and no one to say them to.

I watch Hugo flap, lurching and eventually disappearing around the trees and rocks.

No. I'm not letting this happen.

I scan the beach, my gaze landing on a jet ski.

21

Tyler

The windowless room was supposed to be for privacy, a way to get this deal done and stave off exhaustion. I didn't expect it to be this hard. I was naive maybe—Jax has been in this industry for two decades, and he makes it look easy. I'm used to being able to make things happen myself. Army of one.

"That's it. Wicked's ownership hasn't come back by now, they're not going to." I shove out of my chair.

"If they do and you're not here to sign, this will be over," the lawyer weighs in. "Exclusivity will lapse, and everything we've worked on will be for nothing."

He doesn't say all the money you've spent will be wasted, but it's implied.

A knock comes at the door.

"Yeah," I bark out.

It opens a few inches, and a man appears with a silver cart covered with bottles.

"Apologies, Mr. Adams, we customarily bring a bar for our VIP guests before dinner."

I jerk upright. *Dinner?*

"What time is it?"

He tells me, and the blood drains from my face.

I lean against the wall, flexing my hand. The scars have faded over the past three years since that night in New York changed everything. Now, my eyes crossing from fatigue, the white lines blur.

The image etched in the broken skin—delicate black lines, twisting and weaving—remains clear and steadfast.

The rose, its petals swooping over the back of my hand, its leaves stretching toward my fingers, its vines curling around my wrist.

Annie. She's what matters. When things are going well, but especially when they're not.

Fuck. I'm worried about doing right by artists I don't even know, but I'm not doing right by the most important person in my life.

The truth of that rings through me.

"I need to be with Annie." I roll down my sleeves and start for the door. While the bar attendant hurries to get out of the way, Jax grabs my arm.

He's as frustrated as I am. "Don't make this decision lightly. I know this is the last place you want to be right now. But sometimes the world is bigger than what we want, Tyler."

I suck in a breath, my heart hammering as I step out into the hall for privacy. He follows.

"I get it," I state when I turn back to face him. "You want this deal. You want Wicked because of what they did to you, and you want to shape the industry. But I've been working on something for years too." My throat is raw. "And she's standing out there waiting for me."

Understanding dawns on his face, but I continue. "What would you do if it was Haley out there? Tell me you wouldn't say, 'Fuck the deal.' She's worth a million deals."

He opens his mouth to argue but shakes his head. "You're right. If it was Hales out there, I would give up anything for her."

I clap a hand on his shoulder, then dash down the hallway. As I sprint out the door of the villa, I hit her contact on my phone.

It rings once. Twice.

I hang up as I see Haley stalking up the path.

Her mouth opens, but before she can speak, I hold up a hand. "I'm coming."

I take off down the path, running in the dress shoes I put on during a break between calls.

The sun's setting, and each second feels as if it takes hours.

I'm reckless, urgently needing to be there. Because the stakes are so much higher than a deal.

As I veer off the path and into the sand, my leather soles slipping with each stride, the memory of Annie telling me how badly she wanted to do this at sunset echoes in my head.

I round the last outbuilding, and my chest eases a little when I see everyone there, torches lighting the way.

Something's wrong. There's Harry and Beck and Elle and Pen and Rae, standing with Sophie. Mason's baby stroller...

"Where's Annie?" I pull up, panting.

They're all looking at me.

"She left." Beck's the one to answer, and the heaviness in his tone has cold fear spiking through me.

"Left," I echo. I look toward the horizon, my first awful thought that she's gone from the island even though it's impossible. From the way I grew up, my mind still works in absolutes when I'm panicked—all or nothing. Things and people are gone forever.

"Sophie let Hugo out of his cage," Rae explains. "Annie didn't want him to get hurt, so she's going to the cove." She nods toward the ocean.

"Wait. She went after a bird?"

Annie has a soft heart. It's one thing I love about her, but even though I can't understand this, I need to fix it.

"It's getting dark," says our attendant. "It's dangerous to be out there alone. I've radioed a boat."

"How long will that take?"

"Twenty minutes."

"She's out there," I insist. "Get me a jet ski. A raft. *Something.*" Impatience and panic claw at my throat. "How did you get there before?"

Beck nods down the beach and inland a bit—toward the stable. A string of horses is still tethered outside.

Jesus.

22

Tyler

The water licks at my shins, soaking my pants as the horse picks its way toward the shore. It's dark except for the flashlight attached to the horse's saddle.

This is the last fucking place I thought I'd find myself, but I shove down my discomfort because there's something vitally important I need to do.

Find my fiancée.

I don't curse her out for going after a stupid bird. It's my fault. All of it.

If something happened to her...

No. I won't think about that.

The cove's treeline looms ahead, a dark landmark I fix on as my stomach lurches. I guide the horse toward shore and slip off as we make it up onto the beach. The sand is packed under my feet, firm and steady.

"Annie!" I call, grabbing the light from the horse and shining it ahead of me. "Six!"

No answer.

Her jet ski is tethered to the dock.

Reins in one hand, I stagger up the beach, waving the light ahead.

I've spent a lot of time with this woman in the dark. Searching for her, being with her, wanting her.

Before her, the dark was loneliness, solitude, emptiness.

I won't leave her in that now.

So, I force myself up the beach, searching for what feels like hours. My phone doesn't have reception, and I curse. She must be out here, but knowing she's out of touch and I can't reach her is impossible.

Every inch of beach feels hostile. Every step is darker than the last. I refuse to give up. If I have to search every inch of this island myself, I will find her.

"Fuck, Annie, where are you?" I murmur, fighting the panic.

The horse sidesteps as a gust of breeze comes up suddenly, darting toward the trees. Motion catches my attention, and my breath sticks in my chest.

"Annie?" I call, darting forward.

No answer, at least nothing audible. But I feel her. Sense her.

I head that way, renewed purpose in my steps. The first part of the brush catches at my clothes, the horse on my heels.

I shout her name again.

"Tyler?"

It's small, but the sound of her voice has me inhaling a huge breath.

"Annie!"

The horse grudgingly lets me tug it inland, making low whinnying sounds as if it thinks this is a terrible idea too.

I tie the horse to a tree, my hands purposeful, though they slip on the wet reins. Then I stumble through the low brush, shining the light ahead.

The beam trips over a shape that doesn't look like the forest floor—a glimmer of white. Followed by her face, her hands clutched to her chest.

"Six." I drop to my knees next to her.

She squints up into the light. "Tyler."

I pull her against me. Her body is wet, fabric clinging to her everywhere. Even her hair is damp. I press my lips to her forehead, not caring about anything except that she's here.

"You're so late," she murmurs against my chest.

I attach the light to my belt loop and pull back to

search her face, my eyes adjusting to the dark as I cup her cheeks. "I'm sorry. You have no idea how fucking sorry I am."

She exhales, her breath trembling as she straightens.

A tiny sound between us has me startled.

"What are you holding?" I demand.

"Hugo. I caught him when he landed, but I forgot to bring his cage and couldn't find my way back in the dark. Especially because I tripped into a rock and hurt my ankle."

"Come on." I lift her in my arms and, treading carefully, carry her back out to the beach. "There's a boat coming soon."

I steer us around trees, ensuring I don't bump her into any.

The dark shape looms ahead, craning its neck into the dark.

"You came here on a horse?" Annie says, disbelieving.

"When I found out you'd left, I didn't want to wait."

We get out of the trees, and I set her carefully on the dry sand, the bird still clutched in her hands.

"Wow. Tyler Adams braved a horse for me."

Her half-teasing, half-awestruck tone has my lips

twitching despite the dark emotion that hasn't released its grip on my stomach.

"I'd brave anything for you."

I drop to the sand in front of her, reaching for her ankle. She lets me take it in my hand as I prod it with my fingers.

"You probably think I'm stupid for chasing down a bird at sunset." She winces when I hit a tender spot. "But his mate is waiting for him. I couldn't have him dying before he found her."

The bones feel as if they're in the right places, but she hisses when I hit another spot.

My hands wrap around her ankle, unwilling or unable to let her go. "If something had happened to you over a damn bird…"

Annie sneaks a look out of the corner of her eye. "I'm kind of a romantic. But you knew that when you signed on for this shitshow."

"You're perfect. There's not a single thing about you I would change. But it's good you're holding that bird because otherwise I might kill him myself."

Her half laugh eases the ache in my gut.

"I'm glad you're here," she murmurs, and my chest cracks.

"Me too. I'm sorry I'm late." The breath trembles from my lips, and I stare through the darkness around us, the breeze whipping through my wet shirt. "I'm sorry for a lot of things."

Before she can respond, a light cuts though the darkness from the direction of the sea.

———

"Let us know how she's doing," Jax says at our door, the mask of concern and exhaustion on his face probably matching mine.

I nod as he and Haley turn to leave. At first it seems Jax might not be willing to go, but his wife catches his gaze, and they communicate without words. I pull the door closed as I step back into our villa.

It's been a long-as-hell day. After the boat with Jax, Haley, and our friends arrived and took us back to the resort, the staff doting and worried, we had a doctor check out Annie's ankle. He confirmed it's not sprained or broken, but she's likely to develop an impressive bruise.

Now it's after midnight, and we're finally alone.

"How's it feel?" I ask as I cross back to the living room.

Annie's in the middle of the couch, her leg elevated in the same position as when she hobbled in fifteen minutes ago.

Her face tips up, the lamp in the corner casting a soft glow over her pale skin as her eyes widen. "Terrible. I sprained my wrist falling during rehearsals for the show last year, but this feels worse."

I shift onto the couch next to her, brushing the hair behind her ear, and my lips curve.

She frowns. "Why're you smiling?"

I cut a look toward the clock on the wall. "Because we're getting married today."

Her expression softens, those amber eyes warming.

"Did you finish the deal?" she asks softly.

I bend over to her bare feet, running my thumb along her arch and brushing off the sand that stuck there after she took off her sandals at the door.

"No." My hands move up to the swollen ankle that was wearing an ice pack until a few minutes ago. "Our exclusivity expired tonight, but it doesn't matter." I skim up her calves, the hem of the wet dress.

I work the dress up around her hips, one tiny fraction of an inch at a time, while she sits there, watching me. Her fingers find my jaw, stroking.

She starts to rise, and I shake my head. "Sit."

I reach behind her to the zipper, my gaze on her lap while I work it down. The zipper reaches the bottom, and I slowly tug the dress up over her ribs.

She lifts her arms, and I draw it over her shoulders and head, carefully moving her hair when it catches.

"I'm sorry about Wicked."

I fold the fabric and set it on the end of the couch. Underneath, she's wearing a simple bra and panties that match her skin. I reach back for the clasp and unfasten it.

Annie's gaze is heavy on me, and I feel her emotion from here. It radiates off her in waves, the love, the reluctance. I hate that I've made her question her feelings for me or mine for her.

She's the greatest treasure I've ever found, the person who made me believe in dreams. Each time we were separated was a wound that never quite closed. Remembering is painful, but it's right.

"I won't regret losing Wicked. Not like I'd regret losing you."

I finish removing her bra. Then I work her panties down her hips. I lay both on top of the dress.

I don't linger on her skin, how beautiful she is. The hint of dampness turning into a chill is my concern now.

"You can't lose me. I'm part of you, like you're part of me." Her low voice strokes along my skin, reminding me so much of the words I said to Beck on the plane.

But then I took her for granted. I won't again.

I will spend my life making this up to her. No expense will be too great. Anything this woman wants, she will fucking get.

Before she even asks me, it's hers.

She reaches for my hair, threads her fingers through it, and lifts my face to meet her gaze. What I find there humbles me.

No amount of adoration from fans, no success, can compare to the love in her eyes.

"You'd love me like this if I was still playing studio gigs and struggling to pay the rent, wouldn't you?"

"Every bit as much. And we'd have more time for making Rice Krispies squares."

I reach under her and lift her into my arms. She grabs for my neck in surprise as I carry her to the bathroom.

The huge rain shower is cold, and I step inside to turn on the water and adjust the temperature until it's warm enough to steam.

"You're still dressed," she protests as I help her step inside.

"It's fine."

I wash her, warm her, my hands careful and patient on every inch of her as if all we have is this moment.

Because we do.

When my gaze meets hers as I wash her back, there's understanding in it and a little awe.

I need to do this for her. To be here for her in every way, like I haven't been.

She reaches for my shirt buttons, but I brush away her hand.

"Stop," she murmurs.

I ignore her, continuing my task.

Until she speaks again, her voice commanding enough to make me still. "Tyler. *Stop it.*"

23

Annie

All I wanted was a weekend with our friends and family on an island where Tyler and I could tie the knot in peaceful bliss. I pictured walks on the beach, romantic dinners, couples' massages. Instead, I'd found myself staggering up a beach alone, the rapidly fading sun at my back as I called after a bird as if he knew his own name.

It was dark for a while, but when light cut through the blackness, I nearly sobbed in relief. Tyler was there.

But now that we're back in our villa safe and sound, something's still wrong.

"Stop it," I say again, pushing away his hands.

Since the second he found me, he hasn't strayed

an inch. It's as if he's afraid I'll vanish if he stops watching me, stops touching me.

"This? What you're doing right now? I don't want it," I tell him.

His hands fall to his sides. His clothes are damp from the ocean and from the shower. They cling to every inch of his hard body, the normally proud shoulders slumped. Even in defeat, the man I love is strong and stoic. Tyler's throat bobs, and the emotions fighting behind his eyes make me go on.

"I don't want your guilt," I murmur.

My ankle throbs, but I ignore it as I reach for the buttons on his shirt, unfastening the first. My fingers slip a little, and it takes a second before the fastening gives and I move on. The next button is easier. The third is the same.

"I want your love."

His eyes soften, and the breath that escapes his tense chest wavers at the edges.

When I'm finished unfastening all of them, I spread the shirt wide, pressing a hand against his chest, dark with swirls of ink. My palm lies over his heart as if that's where it's meant to be.

"It's all I've ever wanted from you."

Tyler's throat works, his eyes shining with emotion. He covers my hand with his. "I will be here for you. I'll swear it tomorrow, but I want to swear it tonight."

His words, the low voice, make me tremble. But not with weakness. With conviction.

"I don't need you to be here for me," I murmur. "I need you to be here for *us*. I love watching you create music, and teach, and find your way in the world. But I love you most when you're here with me."

Tyler's thumb strokes the back of my hand. "I want to give you and our children the things you deserve because it's easy to lose everything in a heartbeat."

My gaze drops to his chest. "We haven't yet. And if we do, we'll figure it out."

I lace my fingers through his scarred hand. "We always do. Growing up, I dreamed of being on stage. But mostly, I dreamed of finding somewhere I belonged. I dreamed of *you*. You're my home."

Water runs down his nose and jaw as my hands skim up to cup his face.

He's had to be hard, the man I love. Even as a boy, he had to do things to take care of the few people who broke through his walls.

No more.

We undress him together. The tension that's always between us is beneath the surface, but for once it's content to simmer there.

When we're both warm, he turns off the water and we towel off. He carries me out into the bedroom but doesn't pause there.

"Where are we going?" I ask.

"You wanted to see the stars."

He kicks open the patio door and crosses the stone before setting me on the double-wide chaise lounger and returning to the bedroom to grab a light blanket. Tyler slides in next to me, not hesitating before pulling my body against his.

My forehead rests in the hollow of his chest, and I breathe him in.

"The first time I slept next to you," he murmurs against my hair, his touch stroking down my back, "it felt so fucking right. Nothing in my life ever felt as good as holding you in my arms."

My heart melts. I love him with everything in me.

"I wanted it forever, and I was rocked with the possibility I couldn't have that. It made me keep my guard up, even when we were friends."

I snuggle closer, tracing a finger over the lines of his tattoos. The ship, the compass, the rose.

His lips brush my ear, sending shivers down my spine. "When I thought I might have lost you, I was gutted. I thought I was fucking smarter than that by now. Because if you haven't figured it out... you're it.

You're everything. Where I'm going. How I fight to get there. The reason I try."

We lie like that for a breath. Two. Ten.

The darkness surrounding us feels warm, instead of earlier at the cove, when it was cold.

"They're always there, even when you can't see them," he murmurs. "I used to tell myself that when we were apart. That you were looking up at those same damn stars as me. I didn't know, so I had to believe."

"Now you know it's true because we're together."

I used to lie on the patio at home and wait for the sun to come up. It would warm the stones while I lay there, sending prickles and tingles through my body in a gradual awareness that eventually had me sighing in pleasure.

Now, Tyler's cedar scent invades my senses, and I drink him in. My hands graze across his pecs, carved from hours of the physical work of being a musician.

I sense the moment he feels it too.

"Annie..."

"Shhh." I press my finger to his lips. In the shadows, his handsome face is a dark outline.

I've wanted him my entire life, but the past week has been torture. A never-ending ache just below the surface of my skin. The need for completion, for absolution only he can provide.

We don't need light. It's inside us. Between us.

I lift my mouth to his. I kiss him with everything I am and everything I have—with acceptance, forgiveness, love.

Tyler stiffens a moment as my lips wander, my tongue brushing.

I'm asking him a question I already know the answer to, asking him to want me.

Except he surprises me once again.

Tyler rolls me on top, and my breath catches at the sudden shift. He presses up on his elbows, kissing me back.

Yes.

It feels so damn right.

Here with him, halfway across the world, he's my family, my future. The commitment I've made, the one I will make again.

I trust him to the end of this world and the next.

"Six..." He brushes my cheeks with his thumbs. "What the fuck did I do to deserve you?"

His hands skim down my sides, reverently touching the same places he touched in the shower. This time, his fingers linger. He wants me, and I feel it. He's still holding himself back, his pace steady even as his body hardens under mine.

I let him kiss me and touch me, treat me as if I'm precious.

But it's not what I want.

"Every time you open your eyes, you deserve me," I whisper. "Every time you take a breath. Now show me what you'd do if you believed it."

He stills a moment, then his hand sinks into my hair and he draws me against him, groaning. My hips writhe over his, seeking out friction. He's slick between my thighs because I'm slick, and my head swims at the idea of feeling him inside me.

I try to slip down onto him, and his fingers dig into my legs, holding me off him.

"Not yet," he murmurs, flipping us.

His mouth moves down my body, over my breasts, sucking my nipples until I'm writhing, over my stomach and my thighs, down my calves.

"You're enjoying the stargazing too much?" I tease breathlessly.

"Nah. Let them envy us for a change."

He swallows my laugh as he presses inside me. The moment he does, my humor is eclipsed by something bigger, more profound.

Being connected to him like this, face-to-face, chest to chest, him as deep in me as he'll go, is the closest I've felt to another person. We're so different and so similar, and the contrast is the most fucking exquisite thing I've ever experienced.

My breath mingles with his as his hips pin mine.

He rocks inside me, each stroke a chord he's devoting himself to, part of a song he's been writing forever. One I'd trade eternity to listen to.

I want to draw it out. I need to. But the dreamy haze has its own mind, and it drags me toward a crest I can't fight off. Not even when I wrench my mouth from Tyler's, our lips brushing as we gasp.

"I'm close," I whisper, and his half laugh in the dark makes my heart explode.

"I know."

I know.

He knows me. He knows my body, my mind, my heart. I wouldn't have it any other way.

It's that thought that has me crying out, arching shamelessly against him as if I can draw out every sensation between us, make it a little brighter, a little bolder, a little longer.

He stills inside me, his shoulders flexing, his ass clenching under my calves wrapped around his hips. When he says my name in that beautiful, raw voice, it sends me spinning.

I lock my limbs around him as we tremble together. It's an ode to us.

To yesterday, to today, to always.

24

———

Annie

THE WEDDING DAY

I wake before dawn.

Tyler's still wrapped around me, and for the first time since we arrived, I'm awake and he's still here.

It takes until I shift off the chaise to notice the pain in my ankle has gone down. I carefully put weight on it, pleased that it can bear almost all of me, and go to get dressed.

Excitement shivers through me as I leave the villa, pulling the door quietly shut, and head to the beach behind our villa, needing a moment to myself.

The sunrise turns the sky soft pinks and golds.

It's early, and today is my wedding day.

The anticipation has my lungs nearly bursting. I can't believe it's here.

A man in black is walking barefoot down the beach, but otherwise it's deserted.

A spike of pain shoots up my foot—not my ankle, I realize when I curse and drop to my knee. Just a shell in the sand, scratching enough to leave a tiny white line on the side of my big toe, next to my pedicure.

"You're up early," a rough, masculine voice says.

Harrison King is standing over me, wearing black shorts and nothing else save a faint sheen of sweat as if he's been out for a run. The casual dress contrasts with his perfect cropped hair. His bone structure looks as if it could cut more than the shell I stepped on.

"So are you."

He holds out a hand, and I take it, rising gingerly.

Whatever he does for fitness, he does it with admirable dedication. You don't get in that kind of shape without rigor.

My gaze drops to an outline across his pec—not a tattoo, but a scar. He clears his throat, and I force my attention up.

"I heard about your adventures last night," he

says. "Admittedly, I'm surprised Tyler pulled out of the acquisition. The man has resolve."

I start along the beach, the sand spreading my toes, and he falls into step next to me. "I'm sorry he lost the deal, but I'm relieved there will be no more lawyers on our wedding or honeymoon."

"Deals aren't made by lawyers. They're made by humans. Good ones. Bad ones. Every kind in between."

"What kind are you?" I hear myself ask. I'm thinking about Rae and the fact I didn't tell her who Harrison was at the first opportunity.

Harrison turns to face me, the breeze blowing his shorts. The corners of his eyes crinkle, making their blue depths more piercing. "Haven't you read a tabloid? I'm the rich, self-indulgent, fucked-up kind."

Before I can decipher the emotion on his face, he turns and starts back down the beach.

"You're probably wondering why I called you here," I say when everyone's gathered around a long table at breakfast.

"You want to make sure no one's late today," Beck jokes, and Elle shoves him.

Dad, Haley, Sophie, and Mason are at the end.

Beck's got a shoulder slung over the back of his chair, Rae and Elle on either side of him. Pen's chewing on a piece of pineapple. Harrison's next to Tyler near my end of the table. Even Finn and the other two Wicked artists are here, which is the point.

Tyler shifts out of his chair and crosses to me, his dark brows pulled together. "Six, what's going on?"

"I have an idea. Trust me."

He nods before taking his seat again.

I clear my throat. "We're here together. We're in all of this together. We don't know what will happen with Wicked. But the least we can do is give these artists a chance to do what they do best."

I round the table, stopping in front of them. "Tyler and my dad invited you here because they wanted to convince you they were the best people to take over Wicked. They wanted you to invite them in, but we haven't invited you in, not really. I want to ask if you guys would play at the wedding today."

They exchange a look, but it's Finn who speaks.

"All this for a free wedding band?" he drawls.

Flash, the woman, clears her throat. "I think it's a great idea. It's been stressful as hell not knowing what will happen with the label."

I cross to Finn. "This might be moot at this point because Tyler and my dad let the deal lapse. Because ownership thinks they can get another offer, which they probably won't."

"A company is only as good as its people. Even if you want to go it alone and look out for yourself, there will come a day you need someone to have your back. Tyler and my dad aren't perfect, but they look out for artists in a way executives like Zeke never will."

Finn frowns, looking past my shoulder.

"What if it's not about the lawyers and the fine print?" I turn back to the table. "What if we record it and stream it so the other Wicked artists see it too?"

Beck shoots up in his chair. "Wait. You're going to let me film something?"

"Thanks for taking care of this," I say carefully to Rae as I step into the dress at her and Elle's villa.

"It's just a dress." Her voice is flat, but she inspects it critically, her gaze lingering on every inch of fabric before she tugs gently at the hem to even it.

I turn to face her so when she straightens she can't avoid my gaze. "I'm sorry I didn't tell you about Harrison."

Rae looks gorgeous in a white, sleeveless linen dress that gathers above each shoulder, diving low on her chest. It skims smoothly over her hips and falls to the floor in a soft drape that makes her look younger. The bruises are gone from her wrists, but I still remember them.

"You don't want me to ruin the wedding by bringing it up." She exhales, head swiveling as her gaze searches the room, unseeing.

"Tyler's been wanting to see this guy forever. I thought if I could get him here, everything would be great. But of course, life doesn't work that way. It's not perfect, and I get that. So, if you want to go over there and tell him right now, you have my support. Whatever you need from me, I'm here for you."

Her lips purse. "I will confront him about it."

I touch her arm. "Good. I have your back. I swear."

Before she can answer, we're interrupted.

"Stop being serious!" Elle demands, descending on us with glasses of wine.

Everyone is dressed in white except for me, and I love it. Elle's dress is a flowy halter style. Pen's is sleeveless with a bandeau top that shows off her shoulders.

"Knock knock," Haley calls from the door before entering. She's wearing white too, and Sophie's in pink. My stepmom pulls up just inside the doorway, her hand pressed to her stomach as her eyes fill. "Annie. Oh my God."

Haley's reaction—especially given how rational she typically is—makes my throat tighten.

"It's good?" I ask, holding out the skirt and turning in the mirror.

"It's stunning. You're stunning."

Rae, Elle, and Pen duck out with an excuse about checking on flowers.

I turn back to the mirror, angling my head to see that my hair's still all in place. It's half pinned up and half down, the top portion secured with white jeweled pins that glint in the light.

Together with the dress, it feels like a recognition of the past and a promise of the future. The rich color sends emotion swirling through me every time I see it, every time I touch the silky fabric.

Haley stops behind me, her eyes shining in the mirror. "I still remember the first time I met you backstage at one of your dad's shows. I'd wanted to see you for what felt like forever even though it was only a few weeks."

My lips curve. "Really?"

She nods. "You were the most important thing to him. You still are. There's a piece of his heart nothing else can touch." Haley cuts a look over her shoulder at Sophie, who's playing with a tiny toy truck. "I can't wait for you guys to have kids."

I laugh. "Me either."

Her eyes widen, and I bite my cheek.

"We're not trying. But we're not not trying." After last night, we decided. "Once Tyler's back from tour, he's not going anywhere for a while. And I'll be wrapping up my show. We can stay in New York or move to LA… wherever we want to be."

"That's wonderful. If you ever need a place to stay—"

"With a convenient recording studio and a pool?" I quip, and she smiles. "I know we will. It feels like home for me, and I know it does for Tyler too."

Her eyes fill again, and she swipes at them before she heads to keep a closer eye on Sophie.

I reach for my phone to turn it off. It's filling with congratulations and well-wishes.

I smile as I tuck the phone away and reach for my shoes. I step into them, grateful they're wedges. My ankle still twinges a little but nothing like last night. The doctor was right about that bruise, but I can live with a live bit of pain from the straps pressing in. And the dress will keep the mark out of the pictures.

With one last look in the mirror, I suck in a breath.

I look good. But more than that, I feel good.

I'm going to meet my husband, whom I couldn't love anymore.

There are things unsettled—like the Wicked deal and whatever's between Rae and Harrison. Still, I can set those aside for the moment and focus on the beauty of this instant.

Except...

I frown, scanning the room as I press my hand to my chest above the dress.

"Looking for something?"

My dad's voice has me looking toward the doorway. Relief floods me—both at his form and the chain he holds up.

I race to him. "My necklace!" The chain is new and the glass is repaired so cleanly it's almost impossible to see where it was cracked.

"Tyler fixed it. Don't ask me how."

Dad's gruff voice telling me the man I love saved the necklace he gave me the first summer we were together, back when everything was beautiful and angst-filled and chaotic, has my chest aching.

"Thanks." I throw my arms around Dad's neck. When I pull back, I realize he's wearing a linen suit. "Wow. You look like you're going to bet on a polo match or something."

"Hell no. I'm not going anywhere. Not today. Not

for all the money in the damn world." His face goes slack, his eyes sad.

"What's wrong?"

The biggest rock star of all of them shakes his head slowly, surveying me from my half-pinned hair to my wedge-clad toes under the dress. "Nothing."

My stomach rises into my throat at the emotion in my dad's voice. He's quick to anger, quick to fight, quick to defend.

This version of him is new and disconcerting.

"All I wanted was for you to grow up better than I did. And I might've failed you in that."

I shake my head. "You didn't—"

He cuts me off. "I don't know if I did or didn't. But looking at you, seeing the woman you've become... I want to take credit for it, but I can't. It's all you. I couldn't be prouder, and I have no damn right to take credit for you."

My smile wavers as I touch his shoulders, peering up into his stunned face. "You should take some credit. I wanted you to be proud, always. And I knew you loved me. Even when things were hard between us, when I was angry with you or trying to ignore you or wishing you were different, I knew deep down that you did. That's what made it harder."

"I had a rough patch a few months ago after you and Tyler came for the holidays," he admits.

"What? Why?" I reach for the necklace, and he holds it away, motioning at me to turn.

I do, reluctantly facing the mirror. He loops the necklace around my throat, carefully letting the ring and pendant settle against my chest.

"Because you didn't need me anymore. You haven't for a while. I think taking over Wicked was something I've wanted to do for a long time, but your independence made it more pressing. I want to be needed, but no one needs you forever. I'd never say it to anyone else, but I like being needed, kid." With shaking hands, he fastens the clasp behind my neck and lifts my hair away.

Before he can step back, I grab his thick wrists. His surprised gaze finds mine in the mirror.

"Maybe I don't need you to make sure I eat dinner, like Mason, or tie my shoes, like Sophie," I tease. "Maybe I don't even need your advice on how to play guitar or be a musician, like Tyler. But I need you in my life because you are an example of what is possible in this world. And I need that even in the moments I don't ask for it. Especially when I don't ask for it."

His eyes, the same shade as mine, are glassy.

He wraps his arms around me, and I lean back against him. A sound from the door has us both looking up.

Beck grins. "Sorry to interrupt this beautiful moment, but if you're late two days in a row, Mr. J"—he nods at my dad—"my sixth sense says Haley's going to murder someone."

"You're not really psychic. You just play one on TV," my dad gripes, but he steps back.

"You'd be surprised how much it rubs off," Beck says, then cuts a look at me. He looks a little sad. "You look great, Manatee. Ty's a lucky guy."

I cross to him and stretch up to wrap my arms around him. "I'm a lucky woman. Not only because I have him, because I have the best friends in the world." I pull back to stare him dead in the eyes. "We're not going anywhere, Beck."

His eyes crinkle at the corners. "Come on, stop hitting on me on your wedding day."

I laugh as I pull back and take my dad's arm.

"You've played sold-out shows to fifty thousand. You sure you're ready for this?" I ask him.

"As close as I'm gonna get," he replies solemnly.

25

Annie

The sun is a kiss on my shoulders from the moment I step outside. The breeze tugs at the pins in my hair, my dress.

My friends and family are seated in three rows.

Our officiant is serene up front.

But my eyes are locked on the man next to the altar.

Tyler.

The boy I fell for is a man. One who fills out his tailored tuxedo to perfection, his tattooed hands flexing at his sides as he spots me.

His expression transforms from anticipation to adoration and disbelief.

Memories flood me.

The first time I saw Tyler, the boy with the blue hair and enough talent to steal the world.

Sharing jokes and bands over cheese fries.

Messing around in the studio.

Stumbling into the pool house only to have him pin me up against the wall, an angry, protective god.

The way he went to the prom for me, but not with me. How he carried me to bed after, the way he kissed me as if I was the only thing he needed.

Our first time in college after landing the showcase.

The night he gave me the ring around my neck.

The stage where he gave me the one that's heavy, solid on my finger.

Dad and I make our way up the sand path that's strewn with purple rose petals. My heart is expanding so big I can't feel anything but the tingling and stretching.

I'm a balloon, ready to lift off.

Dad's arm is a support, my fingers digging in as the sand is loose beneath my feet.

My love is tall and strong and handsome. Tyler's face is solemn, filled with love and awe and so much devotion I could die.

I spent my life wanting to be on a stage. This is the only one that matters. Here, with him.

His attention, his caring, his support. It sustains me in a way I never expected.

Muffled sounds have me cutting a look toward our family and friends.

Haley's watching, rapt, pushing Mason's stroller back and forth with one hand as Sophie bounces in her seat.

Pen's grinning, as is Beck. Rae's sitting straight in her chair, a reluctant smile on her face. Even Elle looks charmed for a woman who'd rather be at a funeral than a wedding.

The Wicked artists are there too. Finn nods, one arm slung easily over the back of the chair next to him.

Dad stops next to the altar, and I do too. I press a kiss to his cheek. He cuts a look at the man over my shoulder before opening his mouth to address Tyler.

"I know," my fiancé says.

Dad nods and moves back to join Haley.

When I turn back to Tyler, his attention sweeps me from the hem of my purple dress, to my body, to my flowers, to the necklace, to my face, lingering on my lips before coming to my eyes.

"Nice dress," he murmurs. His lips twitch in appreciation.

"You said once that you wished you'd given me that night. Prom, I mean." I think of our conversation back in college, the longing and the heartache and the regrets we carried then.

"I don't need prom. I've had every second since. All of our past, our present, our future."

My eyes burn, the warmth matching the warmth in my soul as the officiant clears her throat.

She takes us through the simple ceremony we chose. Each word echoes in my ears, my mind, but it's the man in front of me and the family around us —the ones we were born with and the ones we chose —who make this moment beautiful. Holy.

Beck passes us the rings.

"Tyler," I murmur, "I give you this ring as a symbol of my love." I finish the words we were instructed to say before going off book. "But really, you see it every day. Every time I look at you, every moment we spend together, it's a testament to my love for you. We have many identities, some put onto us through blood or circumstance. I've struggled to figure out who I was, but one thing I've always been is yours."

I slide the ring onto his finger, and it settles against his knuckle. Nothing has felt so good.

His jaw tics, those dark chocolate eyes filled with love and anticipation. As if he's been waiting for this moment as long as I have.

"Annie, I give you this ring." His voice is clear and strong, underwritten by so much emotion. "Because giving you rings is what I do." His mouth twitches, and the guests laugh too. "The first time I gave you a ring, I didn't want you to forget me. But that's not enough. You're on this adventure, and all I want is for you to take me with you."

The swelling in my throat is so intense I can't breathe, but I don't need to. Especially when he slides the ring home, where it nests with the engagement ring.

He takes my face in his hands, holding me not as if I'm precious, but as if I'm real and he wants to assure himself of that.

"I love you," he murmurs. "Always."

"Always."

26

Tyler

I don't wait for permission to kiss her.

Since the second she walked toward me in that dress, looking as if she'd stepped out of my own personal fantasy—not a sexual one, though I could make a million of those by fading out the crowd and taking her right here on the sand—but one that belongs to my heart.

For a long time, I was too afraid to want those things because I knew I'd never get them.

But I have.

And I won't ever forget how lucky I am for her. For us. I'll never lose sight of what it means to not only have her in my life, but to share my life with her. The good and the bad, the triumphs and the failures, the choices and the uncertainties.

We can't know what will happen. If we're lucky, we know who we want it to happen with.

I span her waist with my hands, her ribs expanding under my touch as I bend my lips to hers. She's open and eager when I press my tongue against the seam of her mouth.

I dully register the cheer and applause going up from our guests.

"Get a room," someone shouts.

I've been waiting a long fucking time for this.

I'm not the kid I was when I stumbled into Wicked.

I wanted to save that place for the future kids like me, but I also wanted to save it for us. As a testament to our past.

I don't need to. Even if I'm not destined to have a place in its future, I have a place in hers.

Her welcoming warmth, along with the feel of the ring heavy on my finger, is everything in this moment. Her hips are flush with mine, and I want her so fucking badly.

Not because I can't control myself.

Because she's my wife.

I could grace a thousand stages, record a million songs, and none of it would compare to a smile, a breath, a night with her.

Any man who thinks he loves a woman less once he's married needs his head checked.

"When's dinner?" Beck hollers, and I finally pull back.

"This isn't over," I murmur against Annie's swollen lips.

She arches a brow. "I hope not. It's only the start."

I grin because it's true.

Later we're gathered around a long table on the beach.

Nearby, Finn and the others are set up with their instruments. Beck's getting his own footage, zooming in on Finn singing.

At a break, Finn crooks a finger at me, and I excuse myself from my wife long enough to head over.

"Well, never thought I'd be playing your wedding," he says.

"You and me both."

He nods slowly. "I'm putting in a word for you. The other artists are too." He holds up his phone, showing the page with the video Beck shot, the comments piling on it.

"The terms of the deal already expired. It's over."

Finn's eyes gleam. "You'd be surprised."

"Don't tell me you're secretly a good guy."

"I'm not. But maybe I give a shit what happens at that company. Like you said, it's in my best interests."

I suddenly realize what a big deal it was for him to fly halfway around the world on a day's notice.

"I don't think that's it. I think there's something else you care about at that company."

Before Finn can answer, Jax comes over, a strange look on his face. "I got an email from Wicked."

I hold up a hand. "Don't tell me. I'll leave it in your hands. If you want to see it through or not, you have my money and my confidence. I'm out for my honeymoon and until the tour."

Annie's drinking wine and laughing with Elle and Pen. Beck is trying to shoot a video of them.

I head toward Harry at the pop-up bar. "It means a lot to have you here."

"I don't do weddings. But the two of you make it look like something worth aspiring to." A ghost flickers through Harry's dark eyes, so fast most people wouldn't notice.

"Harry, I know—"

"Don't mention it. I have an entertainment empire to distract me. Being a billionaire playboy without a care in the world is a lot of work." The

English accent makes the words drier. He lifts a glass in a smirking toast, and I clink mine to his.

My friend's attention drifts past me, lingers. "Ah. You're in trouble."

I turn to see Annie and Rae watching us, Annie's smile waning and Rae not smiling at all.

"Or you are," I joke.

"Impossible. I only piss off women I know."

Shaking my head, I excuse myself and go back to my wife. "I need to borrow this one," I tell Rae, who seems content to yield my bride to me.

"Where are we going?"

"Dancing," I murmur.

"You don't dance."

"I do with you."

I take her in my arms and tug her across the sand toward the water, stopping short of where the sea laps at the shoreline.

"Do you remember the first time we danced?" she murmurs as she steps closer, her dress brushing my suit.

I press a finger to the necklace she's wearing, the one I busted my ass to fix, before sneaking a guilty look at her face. "You'd better remind me."

"It was a wedding. Dad and Haley's, actually."

"Really?"

"Yes. After the reception," she prods, drawing out each syllable as if it might jog my memory.

"I see." I nod slowly, pretending to catch on. My hands lift to her face, stroking her skin lightly. "The band was playing jazz. I took off to the gazebo, buzzed on champagne I didn't like, and there you were. Barefoot and looking like a fallen angel. One I'd promised I wouldn't touch."

Annie's eyes brim with emotion. "I wished you'd kissed me that night. It would've lasted me the entire summer away from you."

"If I'd kissed you that night, I wouldn't have left for the summer."

Her trembling breath is enough for me to live off. But in case it's not, I brush my lips over hers. She's sweet and edgy, familiar and new, and I thread my hands into her hair to tug her even closer.

We're surrounded by friends and family, dancing on the edge of the earth, and my heart is pounding. Not for them, not for where we are. For the woman in my arms. The one who completes me.

"You're here now," she whispers against my lips.

"We both are. No more excuses, no more take-backs." I can't swallow my grin as I thread her fingers through mine so our rings lie against one another. "It's you and me, Six. Then. Now. Always."

Her lips curve, and I kiss her again.

EPILOGUE

Tyler

"You ready for this?" I ask Annie.

She bends toward the sand next to me, her flowing skirt getting tugged by the breeze as she inspects the cage. "Yes."

The hotel attendants surround us on this important day.

Important, it seems, to my wife, and I guess to the bird.

Annie opens the door, tugs it wide.

Hugo peeps from his cage a couple of times before hopping toward the outside. He twitches his wings a few times before lifting off and sailing into the sky.

"It's a big world," I say solemnly. "Make good choices."

My wife laughs. "You think he'll be okay? He'll find his mate?"

"Let's fucking hope so. Otherwise, he's a goner."

She shoots me a look at my teasing, and I drag her against my side, pressing a kiss to her forehead.

In the week we've been here since the wedding, we've been unwinding a few degrees at a time. Annie's better at it than I am.

One of the attendants' phones go off.

"It's been nonstop since the concert," he says.

Concert is using the term loosely, but Finn and the others' little acoustic session on the beach led to a viral internet presence.

"You're going to be inundated with tourists," I say.

"We tried so hard to hide it."

"Some people still recognized it."

"We've been telling them it wasn't us," the attendant says, smiling.

"It's suspicious given your new merch," Annie deadpans.

One of the women is wearing a tour T-shirt.

Zeke sent way too much, so I diverted one case of

it for the hotel staff, who've been amazing while we're here.

The attendants disperse, and I thread my hand through Annie's. Her ring rests against my skin, and I love the feel of it.

"I have plans for us. We're going for a ride."

I cover her eyes and walk her toward the circular drive in front of the hotel. When I pull back my hands, her attention lands on the motorcycle.

Annie's jaw drops. "Oh my God. I love it." She circles the bike, running her hands over it before her gaze returns to mine. "Where are we going?"

"I have a spot in mind."

I shift onto it, and she gets on behind me. I navigate us through back roads to a beautiful secluded area, complete with protective trees, on a bluff.

"I can hear the fruit doves," Annie gushes. "It feels like we're on the edge of the world."

"I always feel like that with you."

I shift her around so she's in front of me and run my hands down her jaw, my thumbs brushing her lips.

Her slow smile is stunning. "The way you're looking at me might get me pregnant."

"But it might not, so why take the chance?"

I kiss her once, twice, our lips clinging as if the friction is essential. She rubs on me, and I know she's wet under those panties. My fingers stroke up her legs as she hooks them around me.

Every stroke of her hands over my chest, my arms, is heavier than the last, as if stopping touching me would be impossible. When she works my jeans down and I spring free, she licks her lips.

"How's the view?" I ask breathlessly.

"Spectacular."

My fingers sink inside her, and she arches her back as I fill her. She rides my hand as if it's her job. The way she takes her pleasure from me, with the ultimate trust and love, undoes me.

We've had plenty of time together this past week, but so far I'm insatiable. Every second she's not naked in my arms, I'm thinking about what I'll do to make her that way. What I'll do the next time she is.

But I blame it on her too. Every time we come up for air, I'll catch her watching me with the kind of love and devotion I didn't know existed in this world before her.

"Need you," I grunt when I can't take it anymore.

Annie's gold eyes flash. "Take me."

I withdraw my fingers and brush them across her lips. I kiss her hard, tasting her as I position myself between her thighs.

"Bike sex is awkward. They didn't make these for sex," she mumbles against my mouth.

"You'd think. You giving up?"

"Hell no."

I rock into her, my cock finding its way to where it most wants to be. Her body gives, accommodating my greedy demands despite the angle. She gasps, bracing on the handlebars behind her.

I want to last forever, but with her like this, we're already on the edge of the world. It takes nothing to remind me that this is everything.

A dozen heavy strokes and my breath is laboring. The way her hair lifts in the breeze, her nipples puckered through her bra, doesn't help me stay in control.

"All I need is this. You." I press against her clit, rubbing a tight little circle in the way that drives her crazy, and she explodes against me. She calls my name; her body clenches around me, her throat working these strangled cries that make me feel like a god.

Once I've given her every second of pleasure I can, I take my own.

It's unreal every time—because Annie makes me more powerful and more vulnerable than I've ever been in my life.

After, when I shift to make her more comfortable, she asks, "You think I'm pregnant now?"

"At least if you are, our kid will have something. A record label."

"Mhmm, because he or she would've had nothing without Wicked." She shakes her head, smiling.

But I'm a part owner. The deal is going through, with some help from Finn. I guess when something's meant to be, it'll happen in its own time.

"I'm not involved at all," I remind her. "Three more weeks of wedded bliss before the tour."

"I'll come visit you."

"You'd better." I kiss her. "I wish you were coming with me."

"Me too. But I want to finish this show. But for the next three weeks, I'm not thinking of anything but us."

"Good."

I have a few surprises for her. Like that I tweaked the touring schedule so I can surprise *her* at least once a month.

"Until then, can I at least get one of your tour shirts?"

My gut clenches at the soft purr in her voice. "I'll give you one when we get back to our villa. But the second you put it on, you know I'm going to fuck you in it."

"It doesn't seem weird at all that you're turned on

by the idea of me wearing your face?" Annie cocks her head.

"It's so weird." I grin as I hold up our palms, lacing my fingers through hers. "But you're stuck with me now. All my weird is coming out."

She laughs, and I swear I could live on that sound.

When I go on this tour, we'll be in a good place. And I hope she's pregnant. I want kids with her because I know she'll be a great mom. She looks out for those who aren't as strong as she is, she has a voice and knows how to use it, she admits when she's wrong, and most of all—she loves as if it's the only thing worth doing.

Maybe it is.

Annie

TWO MONTHS LATER

I finish my show and head backstage after the second curtain call, breathless and exhausted at once.

Hands catch me in the wings, dragging me against a hard body. I struggle on instinct, flailing with my elbows, until his familiar scent invades my senses.

"Hey, gorgeous."

I suck in a breath. "Tyler."

He's here.

His grip loosens enough I can spin to face him

and peer up into his face, shadowed in the backstage lights.

God, he's gorgeous. Wearing a black leather jacket over jeans, dark shadow on his face as if he hasn't had a chance to shave. He's a fantasy even before I spot the ring on his tattooed hand.

A wave of joy and possessiveness washes over me.

"I was supposed to come to you next weekend," I murmur.

His slow grin is sexy as hell. "I stole a couple of nights off to check on my wife."

My heart swells, my chest aching. "Thank you. But I don't need checking up on."

"No?"

"I'm very capable."

"I know that. But a very capable woman has needs her husband can help her with."

My finger taps my lips as I pretend to consider. "I'm not so sure. You might have outlived your usefulness."

"Oh really? I'll get on that jet back to Sweden, then—"

I grab his belt loop, laughing, and he turns back.

"I have to tell you something."

A few other cast members brush past us, waving at Tyler and exchanging warm greetings.

I wait for them to pass before lowering my voice, taking his jacket in my hands. "I've decided to wrap up the show in three more months. I haven't told the entire cast, but I've worked it out with the producers. I'll be showing..."

Tyler's face slackens, his gaze dropping to my stomach under the costume. "You're pregnant."

I bite my lip, nodding. I took the test a few weeks ago but wanted to wait to see that things were okay and to tell him in person.

His eyes darken, thick lashes blinking. The emotion scrolling across his handsome face is everything.

Then he crushes his mouth to mine. "I can't believe you didn't tell me."

"I wanted to tell you in person."

"Oh, so you're allowed to say that," he teases, reminding me of the day I arrived in LA before our wedding to a roomful of lawyers. "Do you know if it's a boy or a girl?"

I shake my head. "Too early. But since you're here, I'll move my appointment. They should be able to give us a due date."

His grin splits his handsome face.

We head to my changeroom, and he pins me up against the wall.

"It seems ineffective to want to fuck your wife after you learn she's pregnant," I breathe.

Tyler's chocolate eyes warm me everywhere. "This time's for us."

THE WEDDING NIGHT

Nothing this beautiful is real.

The beach, the music, the torches.

My friends deserve every happiness they found today, but I can't focus on it.

"I've never seen a firework display like that," Elle says from her spot perched on a stool next to me at the bar.

"Just wait." I cut a look across the dozen guests remaining since we saw the bride and groom off half an hour ago. They include Jax, now that Haley's taken the kids back to the villa to sleep, Beck, Annie's friend Pen, and the artists from Wicked.

Plus the man I'm here to see.

He's talking with Beck twenty feet away—or being talked to is more like it. Harrison King is tall and broad and fills out his suit in a way no man who deals in deeds and dollars has a right to. His hair, dirty blond in the setting sun hours ago, has warmed in the string lights and torches.

When Beck barks out a laugh, Harrison murmurs a clipped response I can't hear before scanning the beach.

Beautiful. Precise and dangerous, a hunter content to watch its prey until the last minute, knowing he can bring any other person or creature to their knees by saying the word.

Tonight, he's not the hunter.

He's the prey.

He just doesn't know it yet.

I set my empty wine glass in front of the bartender, who tops it up without a word.

"Dude. You're on an express train to a liquid coma." Elle studies me. "Unless you're planning to ditch the dress and streak down the beach on our last night here, in which case, count me in."

"I'm not." I have a plan, and I've been killing time, or nerves, or both until I put it into motion.

Harrison King needs to be held accountable for his company's actions.

A woman was physically assaulted at his club last week, and not a single staff person deigned to intervene.

Not only that, they refused to acknowledge it, burying the incident altogether.

My daily attempts to reach anyone higher up the food chain have failed.

Turns out the man in charge of everything fell into my lap.

This week might've been intended as a reprieve from the hustle, but one thing matters to me now.

Justice.

I turn back toward the bar, glancing at Elle. "There's someone I need to confront. I didn't want to do it until after the wedding, for Tyler and Annie's sake."

Her eyes dance, fascinated. "Really. In that case, I think we need something stronger." She nods to the bartender. "Two tequilas, please."

A moment later, they're set in front of us.

"You're not the confrontational type," Elle says, sliding a shot over to me.

"I am if I'm pissed."

"Cheers to that." We clink our shot glasses, and I toss mine back.

The alcohol burns down my throat, and when Elle begs off to use the bathroom, I make a decision.

It's time.

I square my shoulders and shift off my stool, my wedge sandals slipping in the sand.

I'm tipsier than I thought, my weight falling forward.

The feeling that I'm swimming rather than standing is sliced clean in two by the strong male hands that catch me by the waist and shoulders.

I open my mouth to thank my mystery savior, but the intrusion of a cool British tone has me pulling up short.

"I trust I didn't miss the confrontation."

Fuck.

My gaze drags up the hard body encased in an expensive dark suit to the strong jaw and electric blue eyes.

"Confrontation," I echo, swallowing.

My prey dwarfs me even in my heels. That soul-stealing gaze studies me, insolent. "You told your friend you were preparing to confront someone. So, tell me. What did this person do?"

I grip the back of my stool for balance, jerking out of his grip. "Refused to take responsibility."

His attention drags down my body, making the hairs on my arms lift in the night air and my nipples harden. That attention stops at my stomach. Lingers.

"Congratulations."

"You think I'd be drunk if I was pregnant?"

"We don't know one another that well yet. But I'm relieved to hear it." The smirk on his lips says he was fucking with me. "So, if he's not your lover, who is he, then?"

I'm caught in his eyes, glittering in the firelight. "He thinks he's powerful."

"He thinks or he is?"

I turn the glass in my hand. "He is in some circles."

Harrison shifts closer, and his male scent invades my nose.

It's dangerously refined, like the man himself, reminding me of old money and new sheets.

"Let's go somewhere more private." He tugs at the knot on his tie, and my pulse accelerates.

"What're you doing?"

His firm mouth parts. "Getting comfortable. When a beautiful woman sets out to destroy me, I'm damn well going to enjoy it."

Thank you for reading *A Love Song for Always*! I hope you loved Tyler and Annie's wedding story.

If you want even more of them, devour the exclusive

story **A Wicked Holiday Surprise** - my gift to you
when you join my VIP email list!

https://claims.prolificworks.com/free/9ItBACwD

If you're dying to know what happens next with
Harrison and Rae...

Find out in Beautiful Enemy!

Read a short excerpt below

CHAPTER ONE
Rae

The man across the arrivals lounge in Ibiza is abrasively beautiful. The kind of attractive that could rip you in two.

Which is exactly what seeing him does to me.

Wearing a dark suit, cut close to his strong body, he carries himself with a confidence no man should possess.

No one is that right, least of all *him*.

The man in the lounge turns, calling out to a woman across the room. He's handsome, but I realize he's not the man I haven't been able to get out of my head for the past two months.

This man has dark eyes, not electrifying blue ones. He lacks the crisp British accent that reeks of boarding schools and privilege. Plus, I don't have that feeling in my gut, as if the ground is vibrating beneath my feet.

"I'm sorry, Miss Madani." The baggage clerk's bright voice drags my attention back to the counter. "Your bag was tracked from New York to Heathrow but hasn't shown on the system since."

Her words settle in, and a knot forms in my chest. "That's not possible. I need that bag."

"If we can't deliver it to you in twenty-four hours, you will be reimbursed up to five hundred euros."

I press the heels of my hands to my eyes.

Barely sleeping on the plane, then stumbling onto the next after stopping to brush my teeth and collect a Starbucks grande to get me through customs and the transfer is catching up to me.

I should've known it was a bad idea to put everything I owned in that bag.

Including my pills.

Someone bumps me from behind, and I glance back to see a string of five women in matching white minidresses. The woman at the front of the bachelorette train that was on my plane is wearing a crown and sash, and the train hollers about "one last time."

I'm the only one here *not* looking for a party.

"I understand this is disappointing. A young woman like you, I bet you had your vacation wardrobe chosen." The woman takes in my black tank top and ripped jeans as if I'd do better to start from scratch.

"I'm not here on vacation." I shove a chunk of dark hair out of my face and feel for my crossbody bag, the computer nestled inside.

Thank fuck.

I wonder what she'd say if I told her the truth. That I'm here because I set my career on fire standing up for what I believed in and every venue that was fighting to finger me two months ago is dodging my calls.

When I leave the baggage area, the low-grade throbbing in my gut won't quit.

The company that hired me said they'd send a ride. Sure enough, by the doors is a huge man in a linen suit with graying hair. He holds a sign that says "*L. Queen.*"

"That's me." Professionally, at least. "You can call me Rae."

"No baggage?"

"I wish. What's your name?"

"Toro, señorita."

I fall into step with him as we dodge tourists and head out the double doors.

"Looks like everyone's here to party," I notice.

The people pouring out of the airport are ready to dance and drink and party their cares away.

"And you?" Toro asks.

"I'm here to help them."

I grin and slide my sunglasses onto my face, the warm air washing over me. It was spring in New York yesterday, and now it's summer in Spain.

The ocean breeze washes over me as Toro shows me to a Mercedes limo and holds open the back door.

"I'm riding up front."

Before he can argue, I pull on the passenger door and lift a book off the seat—*Eat, Pray, Love.*

"This your throwback book club pick of the week?" I set it on the dash, and my lips twitch as I cut him a look. "Don't get me wrong, I read it. Upper-middle-class blond chick searches for purpose after her divorce. Found it as relatable as you probably did. Some of us don't need an international journey to find ourselves."

I fasten my seatbelt as he pulls out of the spot.

"Then what are you doing here?"

I shift in my seat under his suddenly curious

gaze. "Dream come true. You mix in Ibiza, you can work anywhere."

But this gig isn't just my big shot...

It's my last shot.

I'm twenty-four years old, and if I don't crush this residency, I might never get another chance to do for a living the one thing that makes me feel alive.

I've wanted to make electronic music since I first put on headphones in front of the computer my parents got me after a traumatic sophomore year of high school.

DJing connects me with an audience in a way that's safe and intimate at once. Unlike other performances, they don't come to watch me.

They come so I'll move them.

There's no better trip.

But the industry doesn't exactly welcome new people with open arms. I've fought with everything I have to get where I am.

Or at least where I was two months ago.

"You came alone," my driver says as we pull out of the airport, and I arch an eyebrow.

"You'd be surprised what a woman can do without a man, Toro," I tease.

I can't imagine being serious enough about a guy to have him travel with me for work.

I'm not blaming my viewpoint on divorced

parents. More like every time life has gotten hard, I've found myself alone.

People leave fast when having your back costs them something.

"I have a grown daughter I haven't seen in some time. She is independent like you. That is why I'm reading the book. My wife said our daughter enjoyed it, and I would like to understand what she likes."

It's so paternal my chest tightens. "She's lucky you take an interest."

"I'm sure your parents are very proud," he says, and I swallow the hard lump that rises up my throat without responding. "I will take you to your accommodations."

"Would you take me to the club instead? I need to check on some specs." Besides, there's nothing I'll do at the villa except stress about my bag.

Toro palms the wheel like a caress. "*Debajo*. It means below."

We pass another venue on the beach side of the road. The sign marking the entrance to the outdoor club is huge, and I watch it in the passenger mirror, a shiver starting in my chest and leaving me tingling all the way down to my toes.

"That's La Mer." I sit up straighter.

People plan their entire vacations, their entire

years, to join the party at one of the biggest clubs in the world.

"I'm going to play there someday."

Toro laughs. "No woman has." He shrugs at my curious look. "My daughter is into EDM."

I slide my sunglasses down and smile, feeling my ribs expand with possibility. "Tell her I'll be the first."

***

Debajo is housed beneath a resort, a fact I forgot until Toro parks around the side of the hotel and walks me to a back entrance.

The underground venue used to be popular but has seen better days, but it still picks up crowds on the long weekends in the summer—like everywhere else on the island.

Toro speaks to security in rapid-fire Spanish, and they let me in.

"Call when you are ready to go to the villa," he insists, pushing a card into my hand as I sling my crossbody bag over my shoulder.

When he's gone, I turn to survey my space.

Everything is industrial, black and chrome. Bars along either side and the stage at the far end of the floor. Booths surround the dance floor. A catwalk overhead wraps around in a balcony and cuts over the middle of the floor, partially obscured by a low, black wall—probably VIP booths.

Two guys work behind the bar, readying it for the evening ahead, while another moves boxes with a cart. None acknowledge me. Capacity is supposed to be two thousand, not that it pulls in that many now.

Still, it's nicer than I expected, and for the next month, this place is mine.

Tonight is the start of something good. I can feel it.

"Damnation."

I jump at the female voice before a woman straightens from behind the setup of boards and sound equipment on stage.

When she spots me, her eyes narrow. "Doors don't open for another twelve hours."

"I'm not a tourist. I'm mixing tonight. Raegan Madani. Little Queen," I go on, supplying the stage name I picked years ago because of its similarity to my given name and because it gave me a persona to build on.

The woman's cropped blond hair has a little gray, but she's midthirties, slim, and wearing a green sundress. A shrewd elf with a tan. "Leni. I run the club."

"And you're American," I say, noticing the accent.

"Hawaii. Big Island, born and raised."

I take the stairs to the stage, then turn to survey the sleek, black Pioneer media players flanking the latest mixer. A lifetime of dreams turned into switches and dials that put power in one person's hands.

"It's had a makeover," she says, noticing my appreciation. "I'm taking over from the previous management long enough to get her on her feet."

"Her?"

"Every club is a woman. Don't think a man could hold this much passion or euphoria. Or this many secrets. She's had a rough patch, though." Leni pats the board but her knowing gaze lands on me. "Must sound familiar."

I bristle, hands gripping the strap on my bag tighter.

"Calling out the head of Echo Entertainment on social media for everyone to see was a dumbass move," Leni goes on.

"A woman was assaulted at their venue on a night I was playing. No one at the club or the organization took responsibility. Harrison King owns the company."

"You knew the woman who was assaulted?"

"Does it matter?"

Too many people ignore women they don't know. I needed to look out for her, even if it was after the fact.

"Let me guess—since then, the clubs that were knocking down your door won't touch you."

I lift my bag and set it on a free spot. "This one did."

I pull out my notebook computer and peer into my bag, remembering my costumes were also in my checked bag. Shit.

"Was it worth it?" she asks.

"Yes." My gaze flicks to hers. "People need to be held responsible for their actions. I don't care how much money Harrison King has. Or how pretty he is. Or how big his dick is."

Her slow grin is feline. "You're the only one. Paparazzi stalk him. Models throw themselves at him. He built an entertainment empire most moguls on their deathbeds would envy, and he did it without a gray hair in sight."

I shiver. From sleep deprivation, not from remembering what it felt like to stand a breath away from that man.

"Rumor is he's hiding out now," Leni replies. "Maybe you hurt his feelings."

"That would require him to have feelings."

Leni smirks as she holds out a network cable. I

lift the lid of my notebook and hit the power key, but the battery's dead.

"I'll never play another of his clubs for as long as I live." I pull the laptop's power cord and adapter from my bag. Before I can reach for the power bar across the desk, a smooth, impossibly male British voice comes from overhead.

"That's a shame. Because the contract you signed says that, for the next month, you're mine."

End of Sample
To continue reading, be sure to pick up *Beautiful Enemy* at your favorite retailer.

THANK YOU

If you read *A Love Song for Always*…thank you. Thank you for trusting me with your time and your heart.

This series has taken me on a wild ride. It's undoubtedly the most raw, emotional story I've written. I'm so grateful for you participating in this with me. I hope Tyler and Annie stay with you for a long time to come. (And I'm not quite done with them yet…make sure you're on my VIP list to get updates on news from this world!)

My readers are the most amazing readers anywhere. You guys are positive, bold, enthusiastic, supportive, and amazing humans. I wouldn't write without you.

If you enjoyed *A Love Song for Always*, I'd be beyond grateful if you could take two minutes to leave a quick review wherever you picked it up. Reviews are like gold to us authors - especially indies.

If you do leave a review, I'd love to hear about it so I can thank you personally. Here're the best ways to reach out:
www.facebook.com/piperlawsonbooks

www.instagram.com/piperlawsonbooks
piper@piperlawsonbooks.com

Thanks for being awesome, for inspiring me every day, and for helping make it possible for me to do something I love.

xoxo

Piper

BOOKS BY PIPER LAWSON

OFF-LIMITS SERIES

Turns out the beautiful man from the club is my new professor... But he wasn't when he kissed me.

Off-Limits is a forbidden age gap college romance series. Find out what happens when the beautiful man from the club is Olivia's hot new professor.

WICKED SERIES

Rockstars don't chase college students. But Jax Jamieson never followed the rules.

Wicked is a new adult rock star series full of nerdy girls, hot rock stars, pet skunks, and ensemble casts you'll want to be friends with forever.

RIVALS SERIES

At seventeen, I offered Tyler Adams my home, my life, my heart. He stole them all.

Rivals is an angsty new adult series. Fans of forbidden romance, enemies to lovers, friends to lovers, and rock star romance will love these books.

ENEMIES SERIES

I sold my soul to a man I hate. Now, he owns me.

Enemies is an enthralling, explosive romance about an American DJ and a British billionaire. If you like wealthy, royal alpha males, enemies to lovers, travel or sexy romance, this series is for you!

TRAVESTY SERIES

My best friend's brother grew up. Hot.

Travesty is a steamy romance series following best friends who start a fashion label from NYC to LA. It contains best friends brother, second chances, enemies to lovers, opposites attract and friends to lovers stories. If you like sexy, sassy romances, you'll love this series.

PLAY SERIES

I know what I want. It's not Max Donovan. To hell with his money, his gaming empire, and his joystick.

Play is an addictive series of standalone romances with slow burn tension, delicious banter, office romance and unforgettable characters. If you like smart, quirky, steamy enemies-to-lovers, contemporary romance, you'll love Play.

ABOUT THE AUTHOR

Piper Lawson is a WSJ and USA Today bestselling author of smart and steamy romance.

She writes women who follow their dreams, best friends who know your dirty secrets and love you anyway, and complex heroes you'll fall hard for.

Piper lives in Canada with her tall and brilliant husband. She's a sucker for dark eyes, dark coffee, and dark chocolate.

For a complete reading list, visit
www.piperlawsonbooks.com/books

Subscribe to Piper's VIP email list
www.piperlawsonbooks.com/subscribe

amazon.com/author/piperlawson

bookbub.com/authors/piper-lawson

instagram.com/piperlawsonbooks

facebook.com/piperlawsonbooks

goodreads.com/piperlawson

ACKNOWLEDGMENTS

First, thank YOU for picking up this book. I love that you trust me to entertain you.

Some of the best love stories take time to tell—time in my life to get it on paper, but more importantly, time in the characters lives to grow up, to make mistakes and learn, and for everything to align so they can finally get their hard-won reward.

That's why Tyler and Annie earned an entire four-book series, complete with an epic HEA. I hope their love, loss, and angst has torn you apart and made you whole again like it's done to me.

This series wouldn't have happened without the support of my awesome readers, including my ARC team. You ladies provide endless enthusiasm, cheerleading, and help spreading the word. I could NOT do it without you, and it would be a lot less fun to try. Extra shoutout to Beth, Tammy and Michelle for the early read! You rock.

Thank you Regina Wamba for the perfect image, and Lori Jackson for the stunning cover.

Becca Mysoor, thank you for your story genius. Cassie Robertson and Devon Burke, thank you for questioning, polishing, and catching all the little things.

Thank you Dani Sanchez for your sage advice and for helping my stories find their way to the right readers.

And Annette Brignac and Michelle Clay... I would not be able to get these books to the people who matter most without you. Don't ever leave me.

Thank you all from the bottom of my heart. The best part of author life is having YOU in it.

Love always,

Piper